EVERYTHING I NEEDED

EVERHOPE ROAD
BOOK 3

EVEY LYON

EVERHOPE ROAD

Everything I Wanted

Everything I Dreamed

Everything I Needed

Copyright © 2025 by Evey Lyon

Written and published by: Evey Lyon, Lost Compass Press

Edited by: Contagious Edits

Proofreading: Rachel Rumble

Cover design e-book and paperback: Lily Bear Design Co.

All rights reserved.

No part of this book may be reproduced in any form or by any electronic or mechanical means. Including information storage and retrieval systems, without written permission from the author, except for the use of brief quotations in a book review.

This book is a work of fiction. The names, characters, places, and incidents are products of the writer's imagination and used fictitiously and are not to be perceived as real. Any resemblance to persons, venues, events, businesses are entirely coincidental.

The author acknowledges the trademark status and trademark owners of various products referenced in this work of fiction, which have been used without permission. The publication/use of these trademarks is not authorized, associated with, or sponsored by the trademark owner.

The author expressly prohibits using this work in any manner for purposes of training artificial intelligence technologies to generate text, including without limitation, technologies that are capable of generating works in the same style or genre as this work. The author reserves all rights to license uses of this work for generative AI training and development of machine learning language models.

Author's Note: No artificial intelligence (A.I.) or predictive language software was used in any part of the creation of this book.

This book is U.S. copy registered and further protected under international copyright laws.

AUTHOR'S NOTE

Here we are. At long last. Sheriff Carter (who first appeared in Waiting to Score) finally gets his story. I was taken by surprise when everyone asked about Sheriff Carter finding love. After all, he was only supposed to be the guy that got set up on an ill-fated date with Violet Dash. But he kept reappearing throughout other stories. Then I realized that his true love wasn't so far away. You've met Rosie Blisswood as a little girl in Something Right, as she is Brooke and Grayson's daughter. She's a woman now… because we never go near a calculator to calculate years when fiction is involved. You don't need to have read any of these stories to enjoy Everything I Needed, but if dots connect in your head when your favorite characters reappear, now you know why.

1

SHERIFF CARTER

We're supposed to be divorced, not end up with our clothes on the floor next to my bed.

That is *not* the thought that should be crossing my mind right now.

My cold gaze locks on the woman on the other side of my parents' backyard that they spend way too much money on upkeep. She still has that smile that is light and fun, her blue eyes always gleaming in marvel, except for the day we said goodbye three years ago, and I haven't seen her since. The light purple dress complements her brown hair that is always lighter in the summer, and it still flows halfway down her back. Of course, she's charming my mother. The whole reason that my ex-wife showed up to my brother's wedding is because of her, I'm sure of it.

"Why is my ex-wife here?" I seethe to my brother, Oliver, who winces in sympathetic pain. He's dressed in a suit with no tie. This is a happy day for him, after all, he's finally having a real wedding with Hailey after they eloped a while back. Then didn't tell anyone they were married for weeks, but meh, to each their own.

"I told you. Mom went rogue with the invites."

My eyes snap to my little brother, wanting so desperately to blame this on him for agreeing to have a wedding at my parents' house along the river. I swear small-town rivers in Illinois, far enough away from Chicago, bring some mystical element to the romance department. But right now, I have bigger issues than scolding the groom on his wedding location choice on this late-afternoon day in June.

"I can see that. Still, why the hell would she show up?"

Oliver shrugs. "Rose and you. Well, it's not like you divorced on the worst terms. I mean, Mom still loves her. Not to mention, she got along really well with everyone in Everhope, and she and Hailey are friendly to one another, too. I'm sure Rose was just in town and then got roped into this. She's always too polite to say no."

Plus, she likes adventure. This is probably a prime opportunity to experience that. It's why we divorced because she wanted to see the world and live for the moment. She's younger that me by twelve years, and I'm pushing forty. I wasn't going to be the one to keep her in Everhope. But I couldn't leave, I'm Sheriff for Lake Spark County, and my life is here. I can't fault her for still believing the world is a wonder to explore.

"It's just Rose. I'm sure she will say congratulations then leave."

Some people call her Rose, but she's Rosie to me. She always complained that Rosie is what she was called as a child and she's a woman now. I would always snort a laugh at that idea and call her Rosie anyhow.

Rosie Blisswood.

It's what she rasped when she first introduced herself. She dropped into my life and knocked me off my feet the moment our eyes met. I was working in Lake Spark a few towns over, and she was there to visit family.

"Fuck, Carter. Just be a gentleman and go say hi. It's not like we have assigned seating for dinner and Mom placed you next to one another." He chuckles, but then it dies and his face falls. Probably because he remembers that Mommy dearest perhaps decided to overstep boundaries again with a smile on her face.

We do love our parents, even if they need to loosen it a bolt or two. They're classic local elite down to their membership at the country club. While Oliver makes millions working in law for the Lake Spark Spinners hockey team, we also have family money. That's why I don't worry about my salary as a sheriff, because let's be honest, I'm not paying off a mortgage with that salary.

My eyes swing back to Rosie, and it's a mistake. Our eyes latch, and her smile fades to a tiny weak one, but still, she doesn't look away. The same feelings I'm having must be stirring inside of her.

Is the disappointment still there? What is this moment that we are about to walk into?

The feeling of a strong hand squeezing my shoulder breaks me away from the spell my ex-wife casts on me.

"We've gotta start this shindig, so if you don't mind, can you figure out your mood for tonight? Stuff a dinner roll or something into your mouth at dinner so you don't say anything you'll regret. This is a happy occasion, and please don't ruin the photos, either." He's half teasing me and half warning me, as he should. Oliver deserves this night.

We walk side by side along the stone path across the lawn, back to the main house where there is a patio full of decorations. The hanging lights are a nice touch. They are going for laidback, which also means not exactly a large crowd. Forty people maybe, not enough to escape certain individuals.

The spot in my chest that was torn out and was only just beginning to heal aches, and my heart begins to quicken. I do my best to stare at anything except Rosie. But as soon as Oliver goes in a different direction and I'm left where the guests are all smiles and chatter, the moment arrives.

Rosie delicately takes a few steps forward, and we both seem hesitant of what to say.

"Hi, Carter." Her voice is fragile, and her eyes drift to the side, but her mouth wears a nuanced, pressed smile. There are not many things she fears. She's the free spirit who had a sunflower in her hair when we went on our first date.

"Rosie." It's a little sharp.

But ah damn, I already hear it in my voice. A sort of swelter that I only get around her, and I'm fucking about to half-smile gently for this woman, and she doesn't deserve it. We were a whirlwind, something that I never expected was in me. I'm structured and she's wild. We were two opposites, but she brought out a part of me that made me breathe differently. I like to think that I did the same to her.

"I was in Everhope on my way back from Lake Spark to see my aunt Lucy and my cousin. I knew Hailey and Oliver were getting married, well, again. I thought I would quickly stop by their house to wish them well. We were all friends at some point."

"And still, you show up here?" The hint of irritation is there.

She stifles a hollow laugh. "I thought I could quickly grab a coffee from Foxy Rox on my way out of town, except… your mother was there."

I scratch my cheek and acknowledge the humor to myself

about the direction of where this story is going. "Let me guess, she was thrilled and insisted you show up tonight."

Rosie bobs her head side to side, and the corners of her mouth curve up. "You know her so well. Then you also know that she wouldn't let me say no. I'm positive she probably would have popped my car tire just to ensure I couldn't leave." She rolls her lips in and quickly circles her eyes around the area to avoid mine.

It takes a moment, but I ease a smidgen. "Probably. She always loved you and still doesn't stop talking about you." As in, she brings up Rosie at every opportunity. It's irritating.

She lifts a shoulder. "I like her, and I'm easy to get along with… I think." Her brows furrow as she doubts herself, which she shouldn't because it's true.

I quickly scan the area and luckily nobody takes notice of us except my mother who gives me a proud little wave before returning to her conversation with one of Oliver's colleagues. It's a shame I'm aware of how one investigates a murder.

A waiter appears from nowhere and offers both of us a cocktail in a mason jar. Eagerly, we both accept one then take a decent swig before our faces wilt from the sourness.

"Is it me or did they go a little strong on the gin?" She peers down into the cocktail of lime, ice, and who knows what else.

"No imagination necessary. Oliver and Hailey were insistent on having a cocktail that they created." I circle the cubes in my jar, also investigating what the contents may be.

Rosie releases a short laugh. "It's nice that they're doing this. I guess when they eloped, they took a page from our book."

Because we went to the courthouse, too. In the spur of the moment, after I bought her a vintage ring from an art market a few towns over. She isn't a diamond kind of girl when it comes to rings.

"Your father wanted to kill me for that move." Even I have to let a light mood float within me.

Rosie shrugs. "Well, Grayson Blisswood is adamant that his little girl still follows his lead and should have had a big wedding at Olive Owl." Their family winery and farm down in Bluetop, not so far from here.

"I'm sure your sister or one of your cousins will have a wedding that makes up for it."

"I guess."

A silence lingers between us for seconds that seem far too long. This should be my cue to escape but my stupid feet remain rooted to the ground.

I remember what my mother cited recently because she keeps tabs on the latest news. "Uh, my mom mentioned that Astro passed. I'm sorry to hear." She loved that horse. Had him since she was a kid and he lived on her family farm.

A shade of sadness crosses her face. "He lived a good life. Not everything can last forever." It feels as though she doesn't mean just the horse.

Which is why her words hit me like a knife, and she must realize that. "Right." My T is a little sharp.

The moment lingers, and for a few seconds, she too seems to be suffering from her own statement.

"So, I guess we should probably go take our seats or something. I hear you have best-man duties," she suggests awkwardly.

"I do. Ridiculously, they have their new dog bringing the rings to them instead. It just means I don't have to worry about losing them."

Her face puzzles. "Is that why there is an emblem of a

Labrador face on every napkin? Plus, don't they already have rings?"

"Yeah, Jet, their dog, is probably more important than any family member. They already have rings and are using the same ones, but now they have something engraved inside of them."

And your wedding ring is still next to mine in a box in my room. It didn't feel right to throw them into the river.

"Enchanting," she replies simply.

The sound of someone clinking a glass brings all the guests' attention, and when Keats, a friend of both me and my brother, announces that the ceremony will begin, people begin to move.

"Well... I-I guess I will see you around," Rosie stammers and shifts her weight to one foot in an attempt to move.

"Yeah."

She nods once and leaves me to watch her saunter away, and I don't think she wanted me to notice how she briefly glanced over her shoulder.

Who the fuck of any higher power decided that I now need to sit through a wedding with my ex-wife not far away?

IT WAS HOPELESS.

The number of times that Rosie and I accidentally locked eyes while the ceremony happened, I lost count.

It's a heavy feeling.

Even the dog running down the aisle only to lie down between Hailey and Oliver while they recited their vows couldn't cause me to laugh.

Am I grumpy person?

Normally not. I enjoy the occasional joke.

Rosie, on the other hand, everything is sunshine and butterflies and probably rainbows and unicorns too.

Now it's night and there are candles floating in my parents' pool. The setting is an extra reminder how two people can be so in love that they celebrate it many ways.

Keats lands himself next to me with a small plate of food in his hand. "Nice little surprise... your ex-wife. Heard it was without warning, too." It's Keats. A coy grin is on his face purely from entertainment.

"Something like that," I duly reply.

We stand side by side and, ah hell, it happens again. My sight gravitates to Rosie who is laughing with Hailey about something. Her laugh trails away when she sees me, and I whip my eyes away.

"Heard you are finally running for mayor since old man Boyle decided to retire."

"My parents have been plotting my campaign for who knows how long with the expectation this would happen. In four years, it will probably be for Congress." At first, it drove me bananas. I thought it was a crazy idea. However, the idea of mayor began to win me over. I would be good at it, and I know this town and county like the back of my hand. We're a small town, and I know city council meetings discuss the most trivial of topics. A new park bench was the last debate. As Sheriff I know everyone, and I'm always updated on the latest town gossip, but I'm behind a wall of law. Mayor would be the same, minus not having to worry about issuing a ticket or throwing someone into jail.

"But yeah, I'm going to do it. I have a good chance, and it's a chapter to add to my life," I explain. Something to partly fill the void that seems present in my life.

Keats slaps a hand on my shoulder. "That's great to hear. You have my vote."

"Thanks." Maybe I don't sound too chipper.

I notice his eyes slide between me and somewhere in the distance to my side. It's a few moments before he tips his head in the direction of Rosie. "Just go walk away somewhere to talk. Really talk. I mean, I saw you before with her and it seemed cozy enough."

I take a long sip of the whiskey that I opted for in place of that awful cocktail.

Keats begins to chuckle to himself. "Well, problem solved." He tips his head in Rosie's direction.

Quickly, I look. "Ah shit." My mother is nearly tugging Rosie along. Rosie seems unsure and is by no means eagerly following, but my mother is too persistent.

"Have fun," Keats mutters as he toasts my glass before he walks away.

"Carter," my mom greets me with a bright lipstick-covered smile to accompany her peach-colored dress. "Look who I found." She almost shoves Rosie at me. "Oh, dear." She pretends to look over my shoulder. "The caterer seems to need my attention. I'm sure you two can have a pleasant catch-up."

Before anyone can protest, my mom is scurrying away, leaving Rosie and me be.

Our eyes both follow my mom's steps in astonishment at her obvious ballsy interruption.

In unison, we look at one another, and I'm desperate to hide my genuine desire to laugh; instead, I present a tight smile.

"Subtle as always," I grit out.

Rosie can't help it and chortles a laugh, ignoring my

steely demeanor. "It's kind of entertaining. I'm happy that I stuck around." She realizes her innocent words strikes a chord.

Without a question, she grabs the drink from my hand and downs it dry. She must be nervous around me.

My brows knit together, and my jaw flexes side to side to lock in my entertained grin. "Flustered?"

"No," she lies.

"Look, I think we can both agree that this was an unexpected encounter today. It seems we can be somewhat cordial, and that's what it is." After all, we grew apart. It wasn't as though some malicious event happened.

"Always the mature one," she retorts.

Lifting my shoulders, I can't deny it. "Well, doesn't always work in my favor." It probably bogged her down, right?

That silence floats back between us.

"I should probably skip the whole dessert table and cake with sparkler. I think I even saw an entire cake for the dog."

"You're crazy about dessert," I point out.

She blows out a breath in an attempt to calm her body. "I was crazy about many things. All the more reason I should probably go." I've never seen her eyes haunted by the past, until now that is.

"Okay," I reply softly. I'm not going to argue. She nods and begins to step away, but I gently touch her elbow to stop her. "Wait…"

I've caved to weakness.

She peers up with wonder. "Yeah?"

"Do you maybe want to catch up for a minute or two?"

Immediately, a faint warm smile paints on her face. "I would like that."

"Don't move." I beeline it to the bar and reach over to

grab a bottle of whiskey when the bartender isn't looking, not that he would care. Returning to Rosie, I hold up the bottle. "Let's go for a walk."

She nods in agreement, and a minute later, the sounds of soft music and conversations are babbling in the distance. I offer her the bottle, and she accepts.

"Heard you were running for mayor. The election is in January, right? Your mom nearly talked my ear off about it. To be honest, I wasn't that surprised."

Rolling a shoulder back as we slowly stroll side by side, I bite my bottom lip. "I keep hearing that from people."

"Because you are a good person," she says, insistent.

I could dispute that it wasn't enough for her, but now doesn't feel like the right time.

"How did seeing the world go?" I ask as she hands me the bottle.

"Okay. I went many places. Got my yoga teacher certification. Even went up to Alaska." Then why do you sound sort of deflated? Disappointed even, I wonder.

"And now you're back to Illinois."

"Yeah," she replies softly. "I'm staying with my parents until I figure things out. I'm already teaching yoga and organizing a few wellness retreats at the winery, also the Dizzy Duck in Lake Spark has asked me to lead a few. I've even started to follow some courses online for combining learning development with movement and art. Hailey asked if I wanted to give children's yoga classes at her preschool, and it will be fun."

It seems she's back in my orbit for the longer term, and I'm not sure how I feel about that.

Quiet floats around us as I'm feeling the alcohol begin to ease me. We pass the bottle between us, and it's probably because we both have more questions but don't dare to ask.

This is when I remember that my mom already let it slip that Rosie is single.

"I guess we might be crossing paths again," I highlight.

"Seems so."

That odd sound of silence returns to us for a few beats until she breaks it. "Look, Carter, I-I… it's just I don't know how to navigate being in the short mile radius of one another again."

I stop and pivot to my side to give her a bitter glare. "We should have thought about that before we signed divorce papers."

Her mouth opens but only a cracked sound escapes. I wince at my sudden harsh mood before blowing out a long breath.

We both face forward, trying to determine if our catch-up is now over. We remain stalled, and I suddenly realize that I didn't take notice of where we were walking. My gaze lifts up to the street sign. My parents live a few streets away from mine.

Unintentionally, we are at Everhope Road. The place where I now live.

The street that our feet seem to gravitate to.

———

I BLINK MY EYES OPEN, and I feel kind of heavy, even though I hit the gym several times a week. The sheets feel loose and twisted, causing me to roll over and investigate, only to find the mattress sheet wrinkled due to someone having lain there.

That's when I sit up, the sheet dropping to the waist of my naked body. As clear as day, I see her.

Rosie is at the end of my bed with her back to me, zipping up the side of her dress.

Oh, shit.

Last night.

"You're running away," I mumble and rub a hand across my groggy face.

Rosie sighs. "This shouldn't have happened. Okay, so we went for a little walk with a bottle of whiskey. We somehow got carried away."

I scoff a breath and appraise my room where clothes are scattered on the floor. "Something like that."

Do we remember what happened? To be honest, it's a little foggy. Only laying her on my bed seems to flash into my mind. We didn't even bother with the lights, instead letting the streetlight peeking through my blinds show us enough. I do remember skating my hand up her thigh as she clawed my hair. Do I recall ripping her panties? Hmm. I swear I can taste her pussy on my lips. I wouldn't have deprived myself of a lick before thrusting into her so hard that it might've caused her to question if it was punishment.

I do recollect that we definitely snapped in a second, moved fast, starving for each other. It was by no means slow. Maybe we were both releasing frustration.

"I'm leaving. No need to talk about this."

I recall a similar conversation before we both signed divorce papers, except she added the sentence that I deserved to find someone that would make me happy.

She didn't get the memo that *she* made me happy, apparently. Instead, she left a bitterness inside of me.

I slide out of bed to find my own clothes. I'm not in the mood to argue. She's right.

"Agreed."

She's finished with getting dressed, and her hair is kind of a mess, but I'm not going to point that out.

We enter a face-off. The tension in the room is unexplainable, but after a stretch of quiet, she gives me one last once-over and leaves.

Growling, I want to scold myself and repeat in my head my original thought.

We're supposed to be divorced, not end up with clothes on the floor next to my bed.

2
ROSIE

SIX WEEKS LATER

My arm hangs off the bed as I lie on my side. Nothing is going to cure this nausea that has made my life hell. Mumbling a sound, I slide my eyes to the floor where a pregnancy test fell out of my hand probably an hour ago when lying down won over the shock because the urge to purge is too strong.

Of course, nothing is going to cure my nausea. Because I have to wait for a baby to come out.

What kind of woman am I?

I broke a man's heart, returned to his life, slept with him, and then got pregnant.

This wasn't supposed to happen. Any of it.

Nobody wants to be divorced, but especially before turning thirty. Nor do I want to feel as though he let me go because I selfishly thought there was more in the world to see, needed to find myself. I haven't figured out if that was the biggest lie of the century or if it might have shaped my personality differently. Carter has every right to hate me, but I'm angry too. So easily, he signed divorce papers without any fight.

Joke's on us. Now, we've circled back to one another whether we intended to or not.

It was just too natural to talk with him and stare into his gleaming brown eyes. He seems to have gotten better-looking with age, and his hair is a little shorter in the back. I should have been responsible and not let us even kiss, but it didn't cross my mind because it seemed that nothing was stopping him, either.

My desire to have his cock inside of me erased logic.

Carter is the man who always brought me joy because I was able to loosen him up, while for the most part, he kept me grounded. Two opposites.

The moment I laid eyes on Carter back then, I knew he would be my husband. It was lust, perhaps. We got carried away because he made me weak in the best possible way. That still seems to be the case.

Now I'm weak for other reasons.

A knock on my door fills me with dread, and the rhythm of the knock informs me of who it is. "Go away, Bella."

My little sister doesn't listen because she has no boundaries. Knocking on the door is only for show.

Bella charges in, and I want to hide the test, but physically I can't move and mentally I give up on the world right now.

"Mom and Dad want to have the weekly Blisswood dinner here next week. Apparently, we've been put on dessert duty." Because that's what happens when you go travel the world and return from your nomad life. You end up living *temporarily* at your parents' house.

She almost skips into the room with her bubbly personality in full force. Bella's home for the summer after graduating college and is insistent the world is peachy because she has her first job in marketing over in Lake Spark for the hockey team.

"Okay." I can barely keep my eyes open because another wave of fatigue and nausea hits me.

She plops herself on the edge of my bed. "Mom also wanted me to ask if you need anything from the store. She said you have a summer virus."

My brows rise, and I smile cynically to myself. "Sure, that's what it is," I mundanely reply.

"Are you feeling alright? You look a little the worse for wear." She begins to rub my back.

"I'll be fine if you go away and let me be," I request, but it's useless, she won't even hear it.

In the corner of my eye, she seems to be peeking over my body to the floor.

Shit.

"Is that what I think it is?"

I don't answer, instead letting her solve the mystery herself when she stands and slowly leans down to stare at the test.

Her jaw drops, and she covers her mouth with her hands. "You're pregnant?" she shrieks.

This is the moment that I push past the struggle and drag my body up to sitting. "Can you keep it down? As in, don't let this news leave this room."

She looks at me, completely confused. "I don't understand. Who have you even been seeing? Is it that new guy who is helping out at Olive Owl, the guy with cowboy vibes?"

I rub my temples and release a calming breath. "Don't ask questions. I'll tell you, but I'm pulling in the sister-oath card."

There is struggle on her face, but she gives in. "Fine." She crosses her arms.

"Carter."

She doesn't grasp it until two seconds later when her eyes turn to saucers. "No effing way. Your ex-husband?"

My palm flies up to stop her. "Yes, now can you just… I don't know. Let me figure this out."

Oh no, that swirl in my stomach is back and traveling up my body. I won't even make it to the bathroom. I lunge forward and grab the small waste bin near my desk just in time to hurl out my peanut butter and jelly sandwich. It's been this way for two days.

Bella watches from the sidelines, completely still, possibly more in shock than I was about an hour ago.

Emptying my stomach never felt so good, despite the sheen of sweat breaking out on my forehead and the fact that I just threw up, but little wins.

Finally, my sister steps forward in an attempt to help and holds the bin as I stand and wipe my mouth with the back of my hand.

"This isn't a drill. That test thingy on the floor is right."

"No shit, Sherlock."

She rolls her eyes at me. "No need to be snappy."

"Sorry. I'm just…"

"Pregnant," she flippantly supplies.

Blowing out a long exhale, I give up in defeat to fate. "Yes."

She sets the bin down and encourages me to come sit next to her on my bed. "What are you going to do?"

"Keep this little vulture inside of me, who is probably cute and will have my button nose and Carter's eyes."

She nudges my shoulder with her own. "Hate to break the bubble, but when are you going to tell him?"

Thinking about it for a few ticks, I don't debate it for long. "I would say I'd wait until I go to the doctor, but it's pretty obvious that I'm 100% pregnant."

"Like, how did it even happen? I mean, I know you ran into him at the wedding for Hailey and Oliver, but I didn't think you two, you know…" She gawks her eyes at me.

"We were drunk or maybe not that drunk. Damn it, we should have used one of those little alcohol measuring thingies, a breathalyzer, that he uses when he is on sheriff duty. It might be worse if we were sober."

"Why? Because you both still have feelings for one another?"

Rubbing my face, I'm well aware that I'm going to need to shower and rinse my mouth, but I can't move yet. "Can you just be quiet for a second? No need to play therapist right now."

Bella stands again and shrugs while walking to the bathroom. "It's obvious," she calls out and disappears, and I hear the faucet, only for her to return with a wet washcloth for me. "If you accidentally sleep with your ex-husband then you need to re-assess if you actually ever had closure."

My chest constricts because a dash of anger boils inside me. I'm mad at myself. I can't fix what I've done, and I'm not going to let a child be the reason that we feel we need to be together.

"Again, save your thoughts for yourself." I pat my mouth, and the coolness of the water feels refreshing. "One day at a time. A reminder that this stays between these four walls. The last thing I need is everyone approaching me with a million questions."

"You have my word. But seriously, when will you tell him?"

I sigh. "Tomorrow. Can I borrow your car? Mine is with the mechanic because they are fixing a light."

"Of course."

"Yippee, telling my baby daddy the news." I lack enthusiasm in my tone.

This baby is unexpected, but he or she will be loved, and that's what matters the most.

Driving on the county road outside of Everhope on this clear summer day, I'm always reminded of how beautiful it is. After leaving corn fields, you drive through lush green hills with horses on one side and the upcoming skyline of tall trees that line the river. I get a little chance to soak in the scenery because I'm not exactly driving pedal to the metal.

I've successfully kept the contents on my stomach inside for an hour more than average, and I can still enjoy wearing my jeans and tank, though I'm aware that it won't be possible in a few months. But still, between nausea and my fear that anything might hurt the baby, I'm acting a little overdramatic, but I'll stick to my fifteen-mile limit.

In my defense, my nerves are also preventing me from concentrating. It's my goal to make it to Everhope and find Carter. I didn't exactly send him a text or give him a call because that would just keep us both in suspense until we talk in person.

It's been six weeks since I've seen him and six weeks where parts of that night have been running on a loop in my head. The moment he pulled his shirt off his shoulders and the second his mouth trailed along the path to my panties. I'm pretty sure he plunged his cock inside of me so hard that I gasped, the way only he can make me feel.

We transpired, but it's something we clearly needed to get out.

Skin-to-skin does things to people, and it's only caused mixed emotions in me since. I replay our marriage, and I question my choices, but then I remind myself that everything happens for a reason and thinking our road ended, but it turns out it was only a detour.

Leaving the warmth of his bed the moment I woke doesn't add any points for me either. It was just too confronting, and what were we going to do? Chat over eggs and coffee? And now? I'm not sure what he'll think of me.

I grab a cracker from the cupholder because I've been keeping a stash there for the whole forty-minute drive, and just as I'm mid-chomp, the sound of a siren hits my ears. Quickly, I glance in the rear-view mirror to see a police car.

Groaning, I turn the wheel and pull onto the side of the road onto the white gravel that crunches under my tires. The light from the police car twirls red and blue in my side-view mirror, and I already feel as though I'll need to offer an overdone smile.

I roll down the window before turning my engine off. I slouch back into my seat and wonder what the hell I've done. It's probably only a broken taillight or something.

I stare at the crackers, the kind with that fake cheese in the middle, and debate if now is the time to snack, but my stomach is a little wavy.

The sound of steps on gravel grows louder until in the corner of my eye, I see a uniform.

"Miss, you're going a little too slow."

No. Oh no.

That timbre is more than familiar.

Just as Carter rests his arm on the roof of the car and leans in, I slowly turn with a lopsided smile. I glance up, and he looks down.

Boom.

We both feel the match that lights tension on fire.

"Rosie." There *may* be a little disdain in his voice.

"Sheriff Carter," I reply curtly. My formality causes a twitch on the corner of his mouth.

"You're back in town, I see." He stands taller and rolls his shoulders back, adjusting to our unplanned meeting.

"Actually…"

Abruptly, he opens the door. "Get out of the car."

Wait, what? "Uhm, why?"

"You know people get tickets for going too slow?"

"I was concerned by a squirrel crossing the road," I lie.

He steps to the side, still indicating for me to get out of the car. Obliging, I do, a little irritated but purely because he's hiding behind that sexy badge and uniform of his and not telling me what he is really thinking for our first encounter since our sex-crazed night.

"Why are you back in Everhope?" He stares at me peculiarly yet with curiousity.

"Actually, I was on the search for…"

Really? Now? This baby decides this is the moment to do this to me? That horrible rolling vomit travels up my body, and I begin to gag. The next thing I know, I lean to the side to puke all over the ground. I avoid examining the ground that has fallen victim to my bodily fluids. My mouth tastes disgusting and the smell rancid. And when I look up as I trudge my body slowly back to standing, I see that Carter's brows are raised with a shade of concern in his eyes but also uncertainty of what the hell just happened.

"I'm pregnant." It bolts out of my mouth completely unplanned, but for some reason, my subconscious decided to just go for it. I touch my mouth as if my lips can confirm what I just said. None of this is going the way I planned.

His piercing brown eyes flutter then squeeze shut, only to open a second later. An uneasy grin begins to drag across his mouth. "You're kidding me, right?" He thinks I'm joking.

I shake my head to his question and remain serious. "I came to tell you. Not like this, obviously." I hold up a finger to pause him when I begin to lurch, only to drop my hands to my thighs as I hunch over, prepared to throw up again, but then it begins to fade away and I'm in the clear. "Phew. False alarm."

"Clearly not a false pregnancy test," he quips.

Slowly rising, I see him with his hands on his hips which brings my attention to his belt with his cuffs. Ah, those were some good times. I snap out of it when I see he is still adjusting to the news I just shared.

Stepping forward, I stop when I realize my instinct is to touch him in comfort. I'm not sure the protocol in this situation.

"We weren't careful."

"Like at all," he intones in agreement.

"Exactly, so here we are." And we should probably question why we were easily so careless.

An unnerving silence wraps around us, and all I can hear is a bird in the distance, an eagle perhaps.

His eyes are fixed on me and then drop to my stomach then zip back to my face. He steps back and laughs bitterly to himself. "Unbelievable."

I don't want him to say it out loud. The irony that he

wanted a family, and I wasn't ready then. Now, when we are divorced, here I am telling him I'm pregnant. What he always dreamed of but now the wrong time.

"So, we're doing this. Having a baby." The tail end of his sentence almost sounds like a question, and I'm disappointed that he thinks he needs to ask if I'm choosing another path.

"Yes," I confirm. "We're doing this." I don't even bother saying to him that he has an out and I'll do it alone, because I know him inside out and he wouldn't run away from this. Not in a million years.

The back of his curled finger wipes his upper lip as he contemplates. "Sorry, but if memory serves me correctly, you didn't want kids yet."

My mouth parts open from his scornful words. "Well, things change. People change." I have a very different view now, and I'm ready to be a mom.

He glances off into the distance right before he steps forward, closing our space, and his hands land on my hips, causing my breath to hitch from the surprise of his sudden touch. My eyes search his and see a man who is fully fueled with his dominant side because of a switch that was flipped ten seconds ago. He walks me back two steps until my back is against the car. In another time, he would've flipped me around and cuffed me in bed.

But now? He's unreadable.

Even more so when his hands move gently, sliding to the side and catching the edge of my tank top to lift just an inch. The feeling of his warm palms rest against my belly, pressing firmly. A tremor runs through me that is purely due to his touch; my body is sensitive to him.

"We're having a baby," he rasps.

My heart pinches with relief and joy, even though we're now in a complex dynamic.

"Yes," I whisper.

His eyes travel between his hands on my belly and my eyes. The smile creeping up on his face could warm anybody's soul.

His entire face brightens, causing my body to release relief and my own elation with this news.

A baby.

Finally, for the first time in days since I started to suspect I was pregnant, I can stop for a moment to let excitement kick in.

"Are you feeling okay? Who else knows? Do you have cravings? When is the doctor's appointment?" he lists and begins to pat my arms, shoulders, and stomach, because clearly he feels he now went to medical school and can examine me. It's endearing, to be honest.

"Slow down." I grin. "Doctor's appointment is in a few weeks. For a few days now, I can only eat crackers now and peanut butter and jelly sandwiches sometimes. I don't think that's a craving, though. It's more my nausea is really bad, as you can see." I gesture down to the ground at our side a few feet away, and we both cringe at the sight of my stomach contents before bringing our gaze back to one another.

"You're throwing up a lot?"

I puff my cheeks before scoffing a laugh. "You could say that again. It's normal. Still, it's how I kind of figured that, well…" I point to myself, up and down. "I'm pregnant."

"Who else knows?"

"Bella. By chance, really. She came into my room when the test was on the floor. I threw up in her presence too, in case you're wondering."

He brushes his fingers across his lips as he seems to be contemplating something, and his face turns stoic.

"Right. You've been living at home for a while."

"Yes," I admit. "Wait, are you still going to give me a ticket?" I joke, because suddenly it feels the moment could use one.

I notice his throat move with a swallow. "No. But you are going to move in with me," he demands firmly.

The entire earth stops.

Because he isn't joking.

3
CARTER

Rosie stares at me, her doe eyes wide in awe. She's probably struggling to grasp what I just said.

"Uh, can you repeat that?" She hasn't blinked yet due to temporary shock.

"You're moving in with me." I'm adamant and with good reason.

I'm going to be a dad.

Rosie is going to be a mom.

The baby is going to be ours.

Unexpected or not, we're both already so deep into the confidence that a baby isn't a disappointment or reason to panic.

That night wasn't planned. This news sure as hell didn't cross our minds as a possibility.

Nor was finding out when I witnessed the mother of my child spew all over the ground before she shared the news.

I should be stuck in shock. Unable to comprehend every word she said.

However, it doesn't happen. Instead, it sets off an instant rocket inside me, and I'll be damned if I don't step up in this very moment to provide for this kid and Rosie. How it's going to go, considering Rosie is my ex-wife, I'm not entirely sure.

She bursts out laughing, and I was expecting this.

Rosie wiggles a pointed finger in my direction. "You're crazy. You know that, right?"

Rolling my eyes, I let her dial down her hysterics while I open her car door and reach across the seat for water and crackers that I see in the cupholder. Her laughter finally dies down by the time the door shuts, and I offer her the refreshments.

She yanks the bottle of water from my hand and opens the cap to rinse out her mouth. Screwing the cap back on, she grabs the crackers and stuffs one into her mouth.

I can only glower at her.

"I'm not moving in," she says with her mouth full.

I swipe the bottle from her hand so she has one less thing to hold on to. "Yes, you are."

"No, I'm not."

"Not negotiable."

Her eyes blaze open, and she begins to fume. "You can't just demand that I pack my boxes and get a key to your house," she huffs then rests her back against the car.

I join her so we stand side by side, and I cross my arms. "Rosie, you're living with your parents. We can both agree that isn't the best solution right now. They will watch your every move like a hawk. Besides, this baby is mine, too. Providing for you is what I should do."

She throws me a glare before floating her gaze back straight ahead into the field. "I'm not an obligation."

"I'm aware of that. Honestly, how did you see this playing out? You'd tell me the news then only see one another at appointments?" I'm doing my best to speak softly to her, not wanting to have an argument. "That's not how it's going to go," I add.

The sound of a grumble causes the corner of my mouth to curve up. It's the tell-tale sign that's she's growing frustrated with me, and we've only just begun our conversation. I used to love the way she stomped and made noises of disapproval. She never could hold up the mood for long, and she would break out into a smile after a minute, only to express her thoughts.

I didn't realize I missed that, but my mind just reminded me that I do.

She nibbles on the cracker. "Carter, we're not going to throw ourselves together because of a baby. This is an unusual situation, and we have to tread carefully. We need to figure out co-parenting, and I don't think packing my car and arriving at your front door is the way to do that."

Now she just lit the sparks inside of me. "Fuck that. I don't deserve to miss all of this. When the baby kicks, or making the crib, or trying to help every time you have to throw up to avoid getting arrested."

She gasps and smiles at the same time. "You weren't going to arrest me."

"No," I agree, but I'm still incredibly frustrated. "We're having a baby. Rosie, think about it. How the fuck are we going to figure this out if you just want to text and see one another at random times. You got your way once, but not this time." My tone could slice through anyone, and shit, I just said what I probably shouldn't have.

Rosie steps away from the car, and I can see the hurt in her eyes. "Is that what you think? I got my way when we got divorced?"

I pinch the bridge of my nose and close my eyes taking a deep breath, well aware that this isn't the time or place for this conversation. Because I could make a long list of why it was the right thing to do. She was young and still had things to discover. I let her go free because that's what you do, right? Sometimes they return.

"You signed the damn papers without much discussion. It was your idea," she snipes.

I'm going to get a headache from this conversation that is heading off course. "Now isn't the time to hash out those details. Not in your condition."

She throws a cracker at me, and I attempt to dodge it. Doesn't matter, my body is hard from muscle, and the cracker just bounces off my stomach, leaving a few crumbs on my shirt.

"Condition? Seriously? I'm not some delicate flower. Next thing I know you're going to tell me that I can't teach yoga or do other stuff." I grow quiet as she plants her hands on her hips. She notices my silence and grumbles again. "You were about to say it, weren't you?"

I shrug my shoulders. "It's not crazy. You need to take it easy, and money isn't an issue."

"Carter, this conversation right now is why I won't be moving in with you." Right, because she hates the thought that I could take care of her ten times over.

Stepping forward, my hand darts out to grab her arm and keep her from creating distance between us, and I'd be lying if it isn't also the need to make it clear who is going to lead our journey forward.

The last few minutes might be a haze on my feelings, separate from the baby. The pain and anger of how we ended and the sudden spark that there is a new chance. I've lost all defenses when it comes to her, and I'm now determined for this baby and what I truly want with this woman, to end the misery that I've been in since we signed those papers.

"Rosie, think of the baby. We have to get it together to ensure we have a united front when this child arrives."

Her eyes drift to my hand on her then back to my face. I notice the way her chest moves up and down. She must feel the current between us, too.

"Right, you have your image to worry about if you're running for mayor," she whispers to herself, but I hear enough.

"Damn it, woman. It didn't even cross my damn mind. Move in. It's the right thing for *us* to do."

"If you are implying what I think you are then you must be well aware that being together purely because there is a baby doesn't mean it's what we should do."

Letting her arm go, I walk back and groan up to the sky and ball my hanging hands into fists purely to tamper my irritation as she watches. "This shouldn't be a negotiation. You came to Everhope to share the news, and it must have crossed your mind how I would respond. It hasn't been that long, you haven't forgotten the way I am."

A few years doesn't erase our memory of someone, especially not the one you would stop the world for.

"We have a lot to unpack, and I don't mean my suitcases," she reminds us both.

"All the more reason for you to move in. We need to figure this out, and it's better that we spend more time together."

Her mouth opens but no words come out because I'm making a solid point. In a few seconds, the bubble of an argument pops, and her shoulders sag while she stares at the ground.

"Carter, I… I don't know how to be around you," she admits in a low voice laced with sorrow.

My own body eases into a moment of truth. "The feeling is mutual, but I'm not backing down on this."

Her lip begins to tremble and her cheeks wrinkle right before a tear pools at the bottom of her eye. "This is a little fucked up."

A car drives by, but we take no notice.

"The timing is a little off, yes."

"Why did we sleep together?" Her fragile voice stabs me somewhere inside. It sounds like regret.

Despite knowing that our night together wasn't the smartest thing for us to have done, I don't carry remorse. I have simply tried to sweep it into the past and move on. Except, I've done a miserable job of it, and Rosie enters my thoughts too many times a day. Having her underneath me again stirred the confusion inside me due to indescribable feelings.

"Time will tell, Rosie. But we made a child, and that's a sign for something."

I can't help it, I enter her space and crook my finger under her chin to lift her gaze to my eyes. No escape. Not anymore. We have to face one another now, tomorrow, and for life.

"Don't lie to me and tell me you don't see it the same way, either," I implore in a rasp.

Her face tilts ever so slightly, but I bring her attention straight back to me and wait for an answer, and I don't need to say anything.

"You're right," she barely whispers.

Finally, I can inhale a calming breath, relieved that we are on another same page today.

We're going to be parents, and this has happened because we're supposed to be tied together. In what way beyond parents, we still have to figure it out.

Her face turns a new shade of pale, and right away, I

bring my fingertips to her shoulders to help keep her standing straight. "It's really bad, isn't it?"

She nods vaguely before pushing me away and crouching over to throw up again. I rub her back and take hold of her hair. She always smells of apple, but admittedly, not today.

The sound of her hurling turns to gagging because it seems she has nothing left in her stomach. "You're okay," I try to soothe her as she dry-heaves.

I did this to her.

My swimmers were insistent that Rosie should have my baby inside her belly, and now she's in complete physical misery.

She keens as she rises again. "When will this end?" She shoots me a warning. "If you say nine months, I swear…"

I chuckle because I completely was about to say that and then point out the calculations would actually mean in eight months.

We have eight months to figure out how we are going to do this. Not just because we are adding a baby to the equation, but I mean where she and I stand. Us.

The rage that I sometimes feel that Rosie left is strong some days, and other days, the hole inside of me begs for her to return.

Selfishly, I'm thankful that she's knocked up with my kid because now she's pushed back into my life, and I have every intention to ensure she's pushed straight into my arms.

Even though she seems woozy, Rosie begins to take a few steps to the car door. "This has been fun and all, but I'm heading back. I'll sleep this off and clear my head. And no, I will not be packing my bags."

I grin to myself because I'm right. She just needs a little time to process the fact that she *will* be getting a key to my place. Or rather the place on Everhope Road where she will forever stay, because I'm a demanding fucker.

"I'm not sure you should be driving right now. Really. That isn't me being a pain in the ass."

She drops herself onto the seat of the car and rests her forehead against the wheel. "Relax," she mumbles. "I'm going to rest and gather strength, then I'll drive back. You go do sheriff things."

"This could all be solved if you let me drive you home… to Everhope Road, so it won't take long, and you can take a nap. I'm off duty now, your slow driving was just an bonus."

She is now exhausted, and I'm positive it's because of me and not our baby causing havoc inside of her.

"Car—" She squeezes the steering wheel, knuckles white, and her mouth closes as if she is trying to calm her nausea.

That's it.

I open the car door fully. "You're coming with me. Otherwise, I swear I will use my handcuffs. Or I can make up something to arrest you for. Now get in my car and I'm driving you to my place."

"Carter." She begins to protest, but I can tell she is no longer physically able to.

"I'm waiting." I hold my arm out to show her that there is plenty of space for her to walk on over to my car. "Come on. Five minutes to my house or forty minutes back to your parents'. What's it going to be?"

The sound of defeat is the only thing I hear when she is no longer reluctant and gets out of the car.

"Oh gee, someone listened," I mock. "I'll come back for your car when Oliver gets home and can take me." The joys of having your brother also be your neighbor.

"Fine." She's a little sluggish, but she heads to my car.

Her telling me she's pregnant doesn't feel as though it

happened twenty minutes ago. Mostly it's due to the fact that I'm already two steps ahead and taking care of her.

I GUESS it's different this time.

It's not dark, and we're not scrambling to get clothes off. Six weeks ago, there wasn't a moment to stop, and Rosie couldn't study my living room and kitchen. We went straight to my bedroom, and the next day, she left as soon as the sun was up.

It's simple but modern, with a fresh feel. Open concept, a lot of white and gray throw pillows. When we were married, we had a cozy three-bedroom off of Main Street. Everything was updated but had more character, she said.

But this house? It's big enough for four babies. Everhope Road? There is an abundance of neighbors and everyone says hi. There is a playground down the street which our son or daughter can enjoy.

I'm already thinking in the future when I need to think in the now.

"I'll grab you a shirt if you want to shower. Maybe you want to lie down on the bed." Really, I say it innocently, but then it feels anything but when Rosie's eyes widen slightly. "In the guest room," I clarify.

"The sofa is fine. I bet I'll feel good as new after a nap or something."

I rub the back of my neck. "Sure. I can find you something to snack on if you think it will help. Toast, perhaps."

She smiles politely at me. "I'll try, but first I need a shower and to clean my mouth, if that's okay."

"Yeah, come on. I'll grab you a towel and bring you some clothes."

"While I'm in the shower?" She's teasing me. To many, it would be flirting, and at least, she's relaxed around me enough to joke now. A contrast to earlier.

She walks past me as if she owns the place, and I follow willingly. "I think I've seen it all."

"True. Soon, I'll be huge, though."

I grin to myself. "With my baby inside of you."

She stalls on a step in front of me. It's probably the way I easily sounded like a man who is proud and protective, maybe even possessive. Not at all borderline crazy.

Swallowing, I feel the need to correct myself. "*Our* baby."

Rosie clears her throat and says no more. After I show her the guest shower, I leave some towels for her by the sink, and I let her be. Being a gentleman, I slipped some clothes through the crack of the door during her shower. In no way shape or form did I glance into the foggy mirror to see the outline of her petite frame and her wet hair cascading down her back as she faced the back tiles.

It took a long breath to remind my dick that she's off limits… temporarily or not.

Once I'm downstairs, I make some toast and leave out butter and jam. She always had this obsession about cold toast. She would always say it's a better way to taste the jam. I never understood it, but Rosie has many quirks. She once burned sage all over the house before letting a frog into the house for luck.

Twenty minutes later, I'm walking down the stairs, having changed into jeans and a tee. "Did you find everything, okay?" I ask as I hop off the last step. I don't get any reply, and my face stills for a second, slightly in fear that she left. "Rosie?" Still no answer.

When I search, I see a half-eaten piece of toast on the

kitchen island before my eyes swing to the couch in the living room where Rosie is sound asleep.

My lips twitch, wanting to smile because she's beautiful. Slightly worn out and pale, but beautiful. It's just the way her hand rests against her cheek or the fact the throw blanket is only covering her middle. It also means I see bare legs and my shirt that drowns her.

The clock on the walls informs me that it's actually dinner time, and with Rosie clearly out like a log, I assume she might actually be out for the night or at least for a solid sleeping session.

Either way, I do something that I probably shouldn't.

I pick her up in my arms, careful not to wake her, and carry her upstairs to my bed.

Lying her gently down on top of the mattress, I can't help but notice something that I missed when re-exploring her body when we slept together, albeit in the dark and drunk, but I notice it now. The tiny tattoo on her inner ankle of a small rose.

The one she got when we eloped because she said roses represent eternal love.

4
ROSIE

How is it possible that I wake up in my ex-husband's bed... again.

I don't even need to appraise the area because I feel the sheets, and my eyes pop open as I lie on my side. The mattress has firmness yet is still heavenly to sleep against. I remember. However, it's the tingle that hits my nose that confirms I'm in Carter's bed.

His scent.

It's not sweet but reminds me of fall, if that's possible. Fall is a warm and cozy season. My favorite, too. Olive Owl, our family winery, is known for pumpkin season, and I couldn't grow up a Blisswood and not love it.

But this smell is fall mixed with Carter. A poison that spreads through my veins.

He is nowhere to be found, which is slightly a relief. I flop to my back, and I raspberry a breath. I turn my head slightly to see the clock saying that it's seven in the morning.

I've been in this bed all night. I don't remember ending up here, nor would this have been my sleeping destination. The sofa was the safest option. It seems that Carter didn't agree and took the liberty to carry me upstairs… to his bed. I should question why here and not the other two bedroom options, but I don't ponder for long.

Nausea is greeting me early today, and I know if I sit up that it will make it worse. Hopeless, I roll to my side, reaching behind me to grab an extra pillow to hold. I've heard many times how morning sickness can go along with pregnancy, but the last few days seem a little excessive if I'm being honest.

I've seen my mom and aunts pregnant, and although they had morning sickness, I don't remember it being this bad.

Escaping this bed isn't going to happen unless I have no choice and need to try and make the trek to the toilet.

My body is stuck in one position with the pit of my stomach moving.

I'd be lying if I blamed staying in bed on the baby. It's probably a little part of me that doesn't want to leave *his* bed.

I'm curious if we kept to our sides or if we cuddled in our sleep. Last time I was here, I woke in his arms. Chiseled muscle with veins visible on his forearms because he's strong and keeps me snug.

The sound of Carter walking up the stairs causes my heart to jump for a second, but then the power of my empty stomach takes over.

His steps slow when he approaches the door to his room. He must be hesitating with what to say. I'll make it easy and tell him the truth: I'm incapable of moving and can only think of how to end this moment of misery.

I don't look up when he enters the room. Okay, I briefly do to see he's in dark blue jeans with a maroon t-shirt.

"Hey," he says softly as he saunters slowly to me.

"Hi," I mumble against the pillow.

His face shows sympathy which means I don't need to explain. "Not feeling too good, are you?"

My eyes hood gently closed in a hope to stop the dizziness hitting my head. "No. The idea of water makes it worse." The crinkle of a wrapper causes me to lift one lid and see that he is holding out bland crackers.

"Maybe this will help." The mattress dips when he sits down next to me and rubs my shoulder as I attempt to sit up before accepting the cracker from his hand. Taking one bite, it seems to help for a few seconds.

Then it doesn't.

I kick off the pillow and blankets, shoving him away, then rush out of bed straight to the bathroom, dropping to the floor next to the toilet, and I throw up clear puke.

I'm not even sure when Carter put his hand on my back and brushed my hair to one side. "It's okay," he says, attempting to soothe me.

It's really not, but fine. I can't get much out, barely any, but the twirl in my stomach is out of me. Relief hits me, but my head feels warm, and hell, I'm worn out.

I'm a ragdoll sitting on the floor, and Carter quickly grabs a towel before he lowers to the ground to be level with me. "Fuck, Rosie, I don't think this is normal anymore."

I wave him off. "I'm pregnant. It comes with the status."

He shakes his head, and his hand shoots out to touch my cheek. His fingers imprint gently onto my skin, and his thumb circles near the corner of my mouth. "No. I'm taking you to the emergency room. Don't even try to debate me on this. You're dehydrated, and what good is that to you or the baby?"

I won't protest, he's right. "Maybe we're just overreacting." I make one last-ditch effort of denial for my current ailments, but he just gives me an unimpressed look. "Okay," I whisper. "Okay, we'll go."

"Thank you for not being difficult and protesting," he says sincerely. "It hasn't even been twenty-four hours since I discovered I'm going to be a dad, and since then, you've only been sick or in a deep sleep."

"You're kind of good at holding my hair back," I joke with half a smile on my dry lips. I go ahead and ask because I'm far too curious in this moment. "Is that why you took me to your bed? In case I needed you to hold my hair back?" I'm poking the bear.

He rolls his lips in and glances away, only to swipe a boyish grin my way. "Among other things." Carter stands and offers me his hands to help me up. "I wasn't going to let you sleep on the couch."

"Still, it's your bed."

I'm wobbly on my feet, and he braces my arms to ensure I don't fall. "If I wasn't concerned then I would jam a cracker into your mouth just to avoid your argument that I did it because I'm trying to prove a point that you should live here."

I snort a laugh. "Where I wouldn't be in your bed, instead one of the spare rooms. Even though your bed is perfect for sleeping."

"I noticed you think so. You slept all night."

My eyes skim to the side because he just casually admitted that he knows because he was watching me most of the night.

And the rhythm of my heart changes.

I'M LYING on an exam table in a curtained cubicle. Luckily, nobody else is in the emergency room, so it's quiet. The crunchy sound of the paper gown annoys me, as I hear it on every micromovement. The doctor smiles as the curtain swooshes open. A woman in her forties enters, and her gaze travels between me and Carter who is sitting next to me before she rolls in a cart with a machine.

She seems surprised by Carter's presence, and for a second, I'm concerned that maybe they dated while I was away, but then I remember he's Sheriff Carter, everybody knows him. I'm sure many tried to set him up while I was away. I always used to laugh because he once told me how years back he had an awkward encounter when a friend tried to set him up with his sister, but she was in a secret relationship with his best friend, who happens to be the team owner of the Spinners hockey team. In my book, ending up with the sheriff was the winner.

"Hello, I'm Dr. White, and I'm from obstetrics. You're in luck, my appointment canceled and I was called down here instead of having the ER doctor come in. Kind of wasn't expecting the sheriff to be here. I heard the paperwork is in for your run as mayor. The head of the hospital board of trustees is running against you, but between you and me, none of us like him."

"Good to know. But Rosie has a little problem right now." He smiles tightly at the reminder.

It takes a moment for Dr. White to jolt into action. "Vomiting. Yes, I understand you've been vomiting quite a bit." She begins to feel my stomach.

I open my mouth, but before I can get a word out, Carter cuts right in. "She's been sick basically non-stop. Even crackers aren't helping. Rosie can't even drink water without gagging. Not to mention, she's weak." You can hear the concern in his voice.

My lips pop because it seems I don't need to explain.

Dr. White throws Carter an amused look before looking at me. "Do you agree?"

"Yeah, it started a few days ago. That's how I figured out I'm pregnant."

She turns on the machine. "The blood tests came back and you are indeed a little low on iron, but I'm not yet worried about anemia. Since you just found out that you're pregnant, you haven't been to a doctor yet?"

"Nope."

"We can calculate from your last period. Or any idea when conception might have been?"

"Yes," Carter and I say in unison.

Dr. White whips her gaze back to Carter and me, probably because we're acting a little strange. "And when might that be?"

"Six weeks ago." Again, by accident, we speak at the same time.

The doctor smirks to herself. "Perhaps Rosie can answer the questions. Just an idea, as she is the pregnant one."

Carter doesn't seem thrilled with that suggestion. "Fine," he grinds out before he sinks back into the chair.

"If it's six weeks ago then you are about eight weeks pregnant. We will be able to see now on the monitor, so let's go ahead and do an ultrasound to check everything is okay there." She's already preparing things and grabbing a wand that she puts gel on.

Carter attempts to get a closer look, and my face is blank.

"It will be a little cold, and you'll feel a little pressure, but we're going to have a look."

I nod in understanding, and then she reaches under the

gown as I lie back and stare at the ceiling, flinching only slightly.

Carter scoops my hand into his as we wait for the doctor to say something. I can feel the wand moving in various angles while Carter seems to be staring at a screen where the doctor occasionally punches a few keyboard keys.

"Well, for sure you have a little baby in there. Also, looks to be exactly around the eight-week mark which means it will be a February baby. I can see a steady heartbeat, too."

Instantly, my eyes bolt to the screen where she points to the little dot flickering on the screen.

Both Carter and I stare in awe.

"We'll have a little listen." The doctor presses a button, and then our small space fills with the sound of a heartbeat.

It's fast and strong and reminds me of swimming under water.

"That's a baby," I whisper to myself and feel the tears forming in my eyes. A beautiful little wonder.

The touch of lips to the back of my hand briefly causes my gaze to shift to see that Carter has our hands interlinked tightly and he kissed my skin. His eyes have a glint of emotion that I've never seen on him.

"Our baby," he whispers softly.

That's it.

That just tipped me over the edge, and a happy tear slips down my cheek.

"I'll print a few photos. It's still quite early, so there isn't so much to see, but when you're back to see your OB in a few weeks then you'll see a more defined shape. But before then, I want to have your lab work done again in a week. Who is your OB?"

"Oh, near where my parents live over in Bluetop," I casually say as I continue to stare at the screen.

"We'll get back to you on that. It's up for discussion," Carter intervenes.

Now my eyes dart to Carter. "Seriously? You're bringing this up now?"

He doesn't let go of my hand and lifts his shoulders. "What? It might be an idea to have your doctor closer to Everhope. You're going to deliver the baby here anyhow."

"Am I?" I'm getting a little steamed right now.

"Okay then," Dr. White interjects awkwardly as she slowly removes the wand. "The file can go anywhere, so you two can figure it out. For now, we should all focus on the fact that Rosie is dehydrated, and I'm going to give her some IV fluids to rectify that."

I prop myself up on my elbows. "Is the baby going to be alright?" Panic hits me.

"The baby is fine. You just saw him or her. But you need fluids, and I'll prescribe some medication for the nausea, too. Try and take it easy. The IV should take a little over an hour, then you can head home and rest. I'll have some information printed for what you can try at home to help with nausea, preventing dehydration, and increasing your iron."

"Sure thing. I'll ensure that happens," Carter intercepts again.

Rolling my eyes, I give up and lie back. "This is going to be impossible."

"What? Call me crazy for wanting to take care of you and *our* baby."

"Okay, well… try to rest," Dr. White comments.

I toss my hands up and blow out a breath. "This is what happens when two ex-spouses decide to make a baby."

"Did we decide? I would say fate just threw this at us," Carter corrects me.

"Huh, so you're Sheriff Carter's ex-wife. Carter's mom,

Nancy, talks about you all the time when I run into her around town. I just moved here a year ago, but I feel like I already know you."

My cheeks hurt from a tight smile. "My former mother-in-law isn't so great with boundaries. Now, we'd appreciate if you keep this little situation under wraps."

"Say no more. You have patient confidentiality. Well, I'll leave you two alone, and the nurse will be in soon to place your line and start the fluids. Try and sip electrolyte drinks and juice on a regular basis. Stick to bland foods. Like I said, make an appointment to come back in for another blood test. Feel better soon."

The moment she is out of earshot, I dagger my eyes to Carter. "Can you stop being so damn adamant?"

He leans in, and I feel him in my air. "No. Get used to it. You're moving in. How else can I take care of you? I doubt saying you have food poisoning will work every day. Your mom for sure won't buy it, which means you have to deal with your parents knowing you're pregnant and not letting you have a second to yourself."

Shoot. He's right.

"Rosie, I'm putting my foot down. When we become roommates, even if I'm on duty I can still stop in to check on you."

"Yeah? And how will that be the answer when everyone realizes that I've moved in with you? Because that won't raise any questions." I'm being sarcastic.

He rubs the stubble on his chin as he now realizes that his plan isn't ideal, either. "Okay, for now it's a little complicated to explain this since we want to keep the news to ourselves. But make no mistake, I give zero fucks what people's opinions might be when they discover that we're having a baby."

Who the hell is this Carter in front of me?

He's out to burn the world down if he needs to. It's some twisted alpha male thing, minus the werewolf or hot guy from *Twilight* part.

Carter is sexy right now but delusional.

We can't just live together at the click of his fingers.

Before I can point out that fact, a new wave of misery takes over my body. "Oh no."

Give the man a treat because he now understands my cues and quickly grabs an emesis bag to hold out right in front of me.

I try but only my stomach moves with nothing coming up. It passes, and Carter combs a few strands of my hair to the side. Since yesterday, all he has done is be by my side. It could be suffocating, but it's comforting not to be alone in this.

A middle-aged nurse arrives with the IV set-up and fluids and a smile on her face. "You'll feel better in a jiffy. How are you with needles?"

"Fine. Just get this over with."

My hand is squeezed again by Carter. "It's going to be okay."

The coolness of the air-conditioning is refreshing, and the feeling of the nurse spreading a blanket over me relaxes me.

"Let's get you nice and comfortable. I assume Sheriff Carter is sticking around." She begins to check my arm for veins. "It's good to have someone with you for this."

"I'm not leaving." He makes it clear to all of us.

I must be halfway through the fluids by the time I feel a dose of energy return. Luckily, we've been quiet. I closed my eyes a few times to doze off, but I'm unsuccessful. Carter continues to stroke my forehead, and it's wildly the answer to what I physically need right now.

I scoff a laugh to myself. "You're really a popular guy

around here. Mayor Carter doesn't have the same ring as Sheriff, though." My voice is still fragile, but I don't want more silence.

"You can call me what you want."

"Soon you'll add Dad to your title."

Our eyes latch, and the ghost of a smile appears on his mouth, and I even have a faint smirk.

"Rosie…"

"Hmm."

"You're physically miserable, but I'll be miserable if I have to watch you from afar." The plea in his voice strikes a chord in me. He sounds like a man suffering and on his knees. His words grab onto me because it's too strong of a sentiment to ignore.

The nurse pops her head around the curtain, breaking our moment. "Still not quite there, but the doctor forgot to give you these." She steps into our space and quickly hands some photos to Carter. "I'll be back soon."

When she's gone, Carter slowly raises the squares in his hands. I look on and see the ultrasound pictures.

The little heart with my name up on the corner along with the date. It says my maiden name Blisswood, instead of Oaks. That's a not-so-subtle reminder that I no longer carry the name of the man next to me.

Yet this baby is a stronger bond than a name.

Our eyes lock and I see it far too well. The promise that he's serious with every word he's said since the moment he found out.

That also means that he won't give up on his idea that I should return to Everhope.

I didn't think enough about how to logistically arrange this pregnancy. It's only been a few days, in which I've spent most of it with morning sickness.

The only thing that is clear is that I wanted to tell him right away. I did that because he is this kid's father, and he has every right to be involved.

He's already willing to jump through hoops to take care of me.

I glance at our baby, then my eyes fly up to meet Carter's.

It's all overwhelming.

But I'm not sure it's why it rolls off my tongue. "Okay." I breathe a sigh of defeat. "I'll move in…"

5
CARTER

The good thing about my little brother living on Everhope Road is that he's my neighbor, and I can knock on Oliver's door when I need to borrow milk or eggs. A bit cliché, but it happens. Living so close also means that sometimes we show up uninvited to one another's houses. We both hold on to an extra set of keys in case we lose a pair, and we know one another's security codes. Then again, I would say the sheriff's house in Everhope is as safe as they come. Nobody wants to get tangled into the repercussion of messing with me.

Since Oliver had to drive me to get Rosie's car the other day, he has questions. He let me get away without a single one when he did me this favor, but that tide has changed, and here he is dropping by for a coffee because I asked for his set of keys.

I come down the stairs to find him already in my kitchen. He grabs a mug for his coffee from the cupboard and drops a pod into the coffee machine before he presses the button. "Why do you need the keys?"

My jaw flexes side to side, preparing myself for this

discussion. Rosie and I agreed that I could tell Oliver and she would inform her parents. For everyone else, we have to take it one week at a time. In an ideal world, nobody would know until Rosie and I figure us out. But that clock doesn't move as fast as I would like.

"I'm not sure that I'll have time to make an extra set, and I need them," I answer.

He raises a brow at me while he adds some milk to his mug. "Care to elaborate?"

"Rosie."

His eyes grow big as he waits for me to complete that sentence. He leans against the counter, crosses his ankles, and begins to sip his coffee.

"She's pregnant."

Oliver nearly sputters out his coffee. "Okay, what the hell is going on?" he asks, as though I'm pulling a prank.

Sliding my hand along the smooth surface of the kitchen island counter, I take a seat on a stool. "Your wedding night. We kind of…"

A slow grin begins to spread on his face. "Sounds like someone else had an exciting wedding night. You're going to be a dad?"

"Yes, you idiot. It's my baby."

"Are you two like back together, remarried, or what?"

I shake my head once side to side. "No." Not yet, anyhow.

"Basically, you two had a one-night stand and she accidentally got pregnant. It happens in life, but with your ex-wife? Uhm, I think that statistic is a little lower," he states confidently before taking another sip.

"That sums it up."

He blows out a whistle and walks to the island and leans over the counter. "She's moving in, and then what?"

I shrug my shoulders and begin to play with the keys that were lying on the counter. "I'm not sure. She's having a bit of a rough time with the pregnancy, just a lot of morning sickness. For now, I think priority is making sure she's okay, and I'll be damned if that happens while she stays with her parents."

"Ah, right. She did that whole wanderlust travel-the-world thing for a while. But you are well aware of that, aren't ya." He winks, and his ability to tease me now hits a little low. Oliver grasps that, and his face turns to understanding and sincerity. "Okay, she's taking up residence here. You think neighbors won't notice? Hell, our parents will flip through the roof. You might actually give Mom a heart attack."

Blowing out an exhausting breath, it reopens the list in my head of what we have to face. "Trust me, I'm well aware. We just need a little time before we brace for that storm."

"Fine, *but* are you going to try and get back together?"

I smirk to myself. "I'm slightly unhinged now. The moment I found out that I'm going to be a dad, it unleashed this part of me that is a little new. Protective and possessive come to mind."

Oliver chuckles. "That isn't new when it involves your ex-wife. It just came out of dormancy for you. This time there is a kid involved."

I rub my face with both hands because hearing the reality out loud is a little rough on the edges. "Priority one is this baby, alright? Everything else has to wait."

My eyes narrow, and I glance over Oliver's shoulder to the wide glass back doors. "Did you bring Jet over? There is a dog digging a hole in the middle of my backyard." This dog is a menace, and I'm not a fan of his visits to my house.

"Don't be cranky. He wanted to see you, and I was out

walking him anyhow. Some people say dogs are calming, perhaps you should borrow him for a while. Your weird-looking trolls on the shelf are not relaxing. They look like little possessed toys that might kill you in your sleep. Especially that creepy ugly Scandinavian one."

Quickly, I glance to the shelf with my bizarre collection that just somehow happened since I was in college.

"Since you're here, can you help move some stuff from one of the spare rooms?"

He places his mug to the side. "Sure. Isn't it a little early to already clear space for the baby's room?"

My lips press together while I try to keep my face neutral, but it's a fail. "It's for Rosie. She agreed to move in as long as she gets the guest room."

The burst of Oliver's laugh could probably be heard down the street. It also causes Jet to race to the door and paw the glass. "*Yeah*, not even going to comment on that. I'm sure in the end it will only be used for her clothes and her yoga mat."

Hopefully.

"How about you stop with the questions and comments. My mind is already about to explode."

He claps his hands together, energized and ready. "Let's do this then."

Oliver and I don't take long to flip the mattress and move some boxes to the other room. I'll put fresh sheets on the bed next time Rosie is here. We haven't set a date, but it will be sooner rather than later.

"Just call me if you need help when she moves. I guess you can't ask Keats yet since he doesn't know. The neighborhood group chat will explode with theories as to why Rosie is here, but I'm sure you two kids can come up with a good story."

"We'll try. It goes without saying yet again, but please keep Mom away."

He closes the cap of the water bottle that he was drinking from and begins to stroll in the direction of the door. "I'm not made of miracles, Carter. Besides, I'm positive that dealing with your ex-wife's dad will make Mom look like a piece of cake."

My lips pinch. "Thanks for that reminder."

"No problem. That's what I'm here for. See ya."

When the door is closed and Oliver walks away, taking Jet along with him, I pause and observe my kitchen and living room.

It's missing a little character. Well, except for the troll with lime-green hair on my living room shelf, next to a few more traditional trolls that are really quite ugly. It's kind of geeky, but that's my thing.

I'm sure when Rosie moves in, in no time, there will be candles and colored pillows and blankets. She probably has a bunch of new items from her travels.

The lack of photos is our doing.

Because we put them away since they were us in a different time.

My phone vibrates, and I pull it out of my pocket in case it's the station. I'm not supposed to be in until tomorrow, but that will only be to handle administration work. The name on my screen causes my mouth to smile wryly.

ROSIE:
Hey. I'm going to tell my parents later today.

I'm quick to reply.

Okay, give me a time and I'll be there.

> Um, no. I can do this myself.

So damn frustrating, her independent streak. I'm a little traditional, so breaking it to her father that she's pregnant by her ex isn't going to be happening solo.

> Yeeeeah

That's all I reply before I grab my car keys because I'm not going to listen to her.

6
ROSIE

Tossing a shirt carelessly into my suitcase, I'm still trying to grasp what I've agreed to.

To move into my ex-husband's, now my baby daddy's, house, that's what.

But in the spur of the moment, I felt that he was right. I don't want to treat this as though we only need to see one another when it's a necessity for the pregnancy. When the baby comes, I want more than basic communication. The sound of only co-parenting in our situation isn't the right label. However, it will take more than a suitcase in his guestroom to unravel our own baggage if we ever decide that we want to be more than parents. The fact that I am even thinking of other possibilities says enough of what I have been harboring in my mind. So, here I am packing.

Bella scoffs a laugh when she pulls out items from my desk to add to a box. I forgot she was here.

She freaked out when I called her to say I was at the hospital and staying the day in Everhope, but she calmed down when I told her I was with Carter. I haven't yet figured out what her thoughts are on my situation, but she goes along with my choices, nonetheless.

"Can I be there when you tell Mom and Dad? I really want to see their faces."

It's not that I'm packing then bolting. It's just that I'm preparing for my move which will be in the near future… or days… day, singular. Almost a shame, really, because this house is great. My dad is an architect, and he designed this house when I was only five. It's big enough for a family of eight, with a pool even. It has everything one could need, except offering me a clue on my current life decisions.

I told Carter that I would inform my parents, and I know they won't tell anyone of my current state until I'm ready. Still, it feels daunting. It might even feel like I'm back in high school and in trouble after sneaking out.

"When are they back?" I double-check.

She quickly glances at her phone screen. "In an hour. They had errands then were going to grab lunch. You know how they are. Still want to date and act all cutesy. It's funny how all of Bluetop looks to them like they're a fairy tale. From Homecoming King and Queen to married. Living the dream."

I give her a pointed look because now isn't the time to hear about happily-ever-afters. "I have to say, this might not be my proudest moment. I disappeared for two days and now I'm going to be moving out without much notice."

"They only want the best for you," she assures me and walks to the window to grab another bag on the floor that needs to be filled.

I'm relieved that the medicine the doctor gave me has been helping. I'm not quite refreshed but almost there.

"Hey, Rosie." She seems interested in something as she

looks out the window and peers down at the driveway. "Uh, is Carter supposed to be here?"

Instantly, the sweater in my hand plops into the suitcase and I beeline it to the window, only to see Carter emerging from his car.

"Oh no." My jaw tightens.

"I take that as a no."

Abandoning the window, I'm on a mission to rip into him. "I can't believe this," I mutter to myself, annoyance on full blast.

Rushing down the stairs, I swing open the front door with gusto and walk straight to Carter who is walking up the driveway and already giving me the familiar look that he isn't surprised. "You don't listen. You didn't get the memo. And yet you're still here." I shove him.

He steps back and raises his hands to let me know he doesn't want to fight, but seriously, what did he expect? "I'm not going to let you tell Brooke and Grayson without me."

I throw my arms up into the air. "We're not teenagers who are admitting that we were irresponsible and now fear that we'll be in trouble." It's only slightly that feeling.

"Really? We were kind of irresponsible on the birth control front," he points out in a humorous way which just shoots my level of irritation up. "We're adults, and all the more reason I'm going to face your dad like a man."

"Honorable," I deadpan, my face unmoved. "Turn around, get in your car, and go back to Everhope. I'll let you know how it goes and when I'm moving."

"Already packing?"

"Yes. No need to check on my end of the move in our bargain. I agreed, and I'm keeping my word. Now, please." My hands come together to pray.

He pinches the bridge of his nose with his eyes heated, but he is contemplating which is something.

The sound of wheels slowly driving up the end of driveway is the last thing I want to hear right now. "Shit." My lips roll in, and my face screws as my hands clench together. It's too late.

My parents are back.

"Well, it seems we're facing them together." Carter raises his brows at me.

With my parents parked next to Carter's car, they both slowly open their doors and hesitantly exit the car, completely confused. It's a wish that I make every day, that I get their genes. My dad doesn't look a day over fifty, and he's anything but, except he has more peppered gray hair. And my mom? She simply looks the same as ten years ago with her brown hair long and her face fresh.

"Carter?" My dad is the first to check the obvious.

"Yes. It's me, in the flesh."

My parents approach us with wary faces. My mom, always willing to smile in most circumstances, nervously attempts to offer one. "It's, uh... good to see you?"

Breathing to myself, I chant inside my head my affirmations of the day.

I accept fate. I have it together. Only good things ahead. My life is not a clusterfuck.

My eyes shoot straight to my dad who hasn't looked away from Carter even an inch as they're in a staredown.

Even my mom notices. "Should we... drinks?" Her voice is uneven. Fair enough. What is one to do when you arrive home to your daughter's ex-husband in the driveway? "It seems we should go inside."

"Let's." My tone is frivolous.

The steely look on my father's face remains as he

follows my mother. Carter and I join the train, and suddenly, it feels like I'm going to be scolded for sneaking out after curfew.

When we're all sitting in the living room, the silence in the room is unnerving. It isn't until my mom sits down on the armrest next to my dad across from Carter and me on the couch that there is a shift in the room.

Carter clears his throat. "Grayson and Brooke. It's good to see you."

My mom's eyes travel between us all. "Let's get real for a second. We have no clue what's going on or how to react right now." My mom is blunt, and she deserves points for that.

Carter and I look at one another for a clue of what to do or who should speak. I roll my eyes because they're my parents, so I might as well take the plunge. I turn my body to face them full-on.

"The funny thing is… uh, Carter is, to *all* of our surprise, here because we have news to share." My words flow slowly out of my mouth.

"Which would be?" My dad's tone is a little stern.

I take a deep breath then feel Carter's hand touch my knee. "I'm pregnant."

Both of my parents are taken aback, with their brows shooting up.

"And before you ask, this wasn't exactly planned," I add.

"Really? Wouldn't have guessed since he is your ex-husband and all." Eek, when Grayson Blisswood attempts to joke when agitated, then it means shit might hit the fan.

"A baby?" My mother seems to be entering some existential episode before a smile warms her mouth. "My little girl is having a baby." Waterworks. Niagara Falls water begins to fall down her face.

It's touching, really. Actually, it's a relief. Even as an adult you don't want to disappoint your parents.

My vision swings to my dad whose lips suddenly in a smile. "This is wonderful news. I mean, being grandparents is a little rough on the age confrontation, but you're going to have a baby."

"Yeah… yeah, I am." My voice feathers, and I'm suddenly proud, a smile beaming on my face.

"Obviously, I'm going to take care of Rosie and the baby," Carter clarifies.

The smiles that my family have decrease in size, and their knitted brows return, as they're puzzled. "Right. So, maybe we can backtrack a sec, and update us on why my ex-son-in-law is sitting on my couch. Because, I mean, I'm thrilled it's Carter who is going to be this kid's dad."

"Really? Could've fooled me two minutes ago when you were contemplating options of poison," I deadpan.

My father laughs me off. "Hey, I didn't know why he was here. I'm protective." He shrugs.

Wiping away a tear, my mom touches my dad's leg. "This is really great news. I mean, they're back together, which is just fantastic." Because they were Carter superfans.

Pop goes the happy bubble.

"Not exactly," I say to dampen the mood.

Carter scoots closer to me. "Rosie is moving in with me, and we're taking it one day at a time."

My dad points to us with confidence. "Nah, your mom and I parted ways for a while, and then we found one another again when Rosie was young. You two will be fine," he easily voices his views.

A slight wave of nausea surfaces, and I swallow in the hopes that it helps.

"You okay?" Carter is quick to jump in with concern.

I claw my nails into his leg to hang on. "Yep," I struggle to say.

My mom stands with urgency and zips straight to me at the speed of light. "Morning sickness? I had it really bad with you. You need to eat raw ginger." She begins to cradle my head to rest against her stomach as if I'm a toddler.

"It will go away, they say. I'm now nine weeks."

"We wanted to tell you even though it's early."

My parents seem taken aback and glance at one another. "Oh, well, makes sense. Work on you two before the baby arrives," my father says.

"For fuck's sake." I pull back from my mom's hands.

"Language," my dad chides.

"Will everyone just calm it down on the relationship views? We have bigger things to conquer right now, which is this adorable little demon in my stomach making me sick half the time."

Carter begins to rub my back. "The ER doctor gave her meds to help."

"What?" my mom shrieks.

"Way to go," I utter to Carter.

"You were at the hospital? That's it. You're staying here. You need me with you." She's probably already planning my breakfast menu for the week in her head.

I abruptly stand, completely exhausted from all of this. "I'm going to live with Carter. I need to figure everything out. I don't want to be coddled. Not by you, Mom, or you." I dart my eyes to Carter. "Just let me be. I need to wrap my head around a few things."

"Of course." My dad grabs my mom's wrist to rein her in. "You two should rely on one another right now."

"This discussion is finished. You're both aware now, and I'll be at another address until further notice by the end of the week." I pivot on my feet and nearly march to the front door while Carter says goodbye, and then he is outside with me.

My arms are crossed and my feet firm on the cement. It's when the feeling of the hand that has always been comforting touches my shoulder and guides me to turn to face him, that I realize why I'm about to melt down.

Everybody loves Carter. Everyone thinks I made a mistake when we parted ways. That's what it has to be. They're all ready to welcome him back with open arms because this is a chance to repair what never should have been broken.

It's the worst possible time to do this, especially with eyes probably on us, but I can't help it. I'm emotional, and my eyes sting from tears because of the whole situation and I'm overwhelmed. I dive my face into Carter's chest, feeling his arms slowly wrap around me to hold me closer.

I don't think I can blame this on pregnancy hormones. It's simply life throwing me a sign.

"Shh, it's okay." His whisper always does things to my body. Sometimes sending sensations that come down to passion, and sometimes it glues to my spine, keeping me firm to the ground.

A tear releases. "Carter, I'm so tired and scared and exhausted... I'll move tomorrow."

I hear his audible breath of relief. "The guestroom awaits you... I do, too." I'm not sure I was meant to hear that.

But I did.

7
CARTER

Rosie is sitting on the step in front of my house, hunched forward as she leans against her knees where her dark fingernails tap, her braid to the side perfectly set. Her scowl would be concerning if it wasn't for the fact that I can see that it's a façade because she's horrible at pretending. I was married to her. You learn every little detail of someone.

The sun is out, which adds to the sheen of sweat for my workout of carrying boxes and luggage into my house. Every time I pass her, her eyes follow me.

As I'm pulling out another box, she seems to shift in her watch post. "Are you sure I can't at least grab something? This is ridiculous."

I stop mid box pull from her trunk and quickly flash her a pointed look, and at last her dampened smile breaks out. "Rosie..." I quickly look around to ensure nobody is around to hear. "You're pregnant. Over my dead body are you carrying this stuff inside. I let you carry your yoga mat and that's all you will be doing."

"Fine," she huffs.

I'm relieved she's been feeling a little better. More tired than sick, although her stomach wooziness comes and goes.

"This is the last of it, anyhow."

Holding the box in one hand, I shut the trunk. Walking back into the house, Rosie joins me. I drop the box by the bottom of the stairs and opt for a little break.

She goes to the kitchen without me saying a word about how I need a drink. She has brisk steps, and all I can do is follow her with my lips rolled in and fighting a grin.

Noticing that she's already grabbing two glasses, I lean against the counter and watch her pull out a pitcher of iced tea that she then pours into the glasses. My lips are sealed because she may throw something at me if I point out that she's already made herself at home.

She sticks her arm out and offers me a glass. "Here."

"Thank you."

She takes a small sip then smacks her lips, causing her wince. "This tastes weird."

"Tastes fine to me."

"Ugh. Another thing to add to my list of side effects of a reckless night. My sense of taste has gone haywire," she complains with a lightened tone.

"Reckless?" My brows rise from her brazen choice of definition.

She rolls her eyes to the side and her cheeks tighten from her own humor. "We're going to have to revisit what to call it one day."

Enjoying another sip, I'm not worried. "That's going to be a fun conversation," I answer dryly.

She sputters a laugh. "True." Her focus changes to something else, and she searches my kitchen with her gaze. "Maybe I should try eating something."

"There are some cookies in the jar over there." I indicate

with my nose. She is quick to lift the lid, but I have to stop her. "Not that one. Those are Jet's treats."

Her jaw goes slack before she grins with her soft pink lips. "I thought you can't stand that dog. Someone mentioned it at the wedding, and then you pointed out to me why there are holes all over the garden when you gave me the grand tour earlier." I do my best to avoid her gaze. "Ooh, somebody has a soft spot," Rosie sings and slides the jar to the side. "Don't worry. Your secret is safe with me."

I roll a shoulder back. "It's more to throw over the fence and get him out of my yard kind of thing. He sometimes wanders here."

"Sure. Keep telling yourself that." She pops the lid on the cookie jar and then her smile fades to affection as she picks up a cookie. "Pink wafers."

Scratching my stubble, I try to downplay this. "Yeah, you mentioned the other week about having a craving for them."

Lines form on her forehead. "For like a millisecond, I mentioned." She holds up the cookie with a half-smile before taking a big bite. "Thank you. It's exactly what I need." Her mouth is full, but I got the gist.

"Just say what you need, and I'll get it at the grocery store."

She brushes a crumb from her mouth. "I can handle the grocery store on my own."

"I know. Just thought with your morning sickness and smells and town gossip that maybe you would want to hide out a little."

"I think I'll be okay the next few days. Gracie is living in Everhope now." My second cousin. "Plus, I'll head down the street to see Esme and Hailey." Esme is married to Keats, and she's also another neighbor on Everhope Road.

"They won't ask much if I say not to. Then I'm another

week gone and almost to the twelve-week mark by the time the town realizes I'm really back, and then give it another few weeks before they discover the baby news. We can handle it all in waves."

My lips quirk out, and I tilt my head to the side from her logic, and it makes sense. "We can give that a try. It's just, well, my mom requires a different plan."

"Ah shoot, you're right. We need an entire wall to work out a map and project scope of how to handle her," she teases me. "I'm well aware that Nancy Oaks will be the biggest obstacle of them all. But I don't want to think about that now. Do you mind if I start to unpack?"

"Sure. I'll help with the heavy stuff." I gesture lazily behind me to the living room. "I'm going to take a wild guess that the tea set, incense, pillows, and basket of yoga supplies will find a place in the living room."

She seems to enjoy the fact that I'm right and grimaces to herself. "It would be kind of odd to bring out the old photos of us, so yes. We will be sticking to simple objects."

Gently, I shake my head at her humor before we head upstairs.

The moment she's in the room, she hops onto the bed then feels the duvet with the palm of her hand.

"Comfy."

Standing in the doorway, I watch her, realizing she's under my roof but in the wrong bed. I swallow and inhale a long breath because I can't think that.

"I wouldn't know. I have a bedroom not so far from here." And fuck me, I just did what I said I couldn't think about. Worse is that I had a flirty tone.

Rosie wiggles her finger side to side at me. "I'll be staying here in this bed for a while." Her jaw sets to the side when she realizes that *a while* can be perceived as a temporary time.

Neither of us say anything, and we begin to search the room frantically for something to occupy us. Clearing my throat, I step forward and pick up her laptop bag to set on the dresser.

"Just make yourself at home. Do what you want with the room, the kitchen, living room, hell, wherever."

"Of course." She grabs a quilt, the one her aunts made for her when she was in college, and throws it onto the bed. "The, uh, other spare rooms. I mean, it's extra space, and the baby will need to take up residence somewhere. It's just that it's a little permanent on the future front. Maybe we can address that issue when it's time to figure out the living situation and which room to decorate as a nursery, and hopefully a nursery is needed in only one house… mine." She avoids my eyes.

It's a fair point, even if there is an obvious answer for me. "Don't worry yourself with it right now. Just take it easy."

She offers me an appreciative look. "That sounds good." Rosie kicks her sandals off and crawls back until her head lands on the mound of pillows. "Maybe I'll take a little power nap before conquering all of this."

"Good idea. I'll help you later."

"Thanks."

I let her be but return a few minutes later when I realize I forgot to give her towels. I sneak in to set them in the bathroom but pause when I exit. I take a moment to take in the view of Rosie sleeping with one leg bent and her hands by her head. Maybe pregnancy is making her more beautiful, but she has a glow.

Deciding that I can't lurk and watch her all day, I turn my feet to leave, only to see that two stacked boxes are stacked crooked and might fall. I decide to quietly shift them but fail when one box drops. I curse to myself and glance up, but Rosie barely stirs and seems to be deep in sleep. It wasn't loud since the box is light.

Leaning down to pick it up, one flap is loose, and my eyes drive down to see the contents, and instantly my entire body tugs.

There is an array of troll figures on the floor. Some with different vibrant-colored hair and others more traditional trolls with ugly faces or dressed in national costumes. Anyone would laugh because it's a funny thing to collect.

Leaning down, I slowly pick up the one in a fur parka with Alaska written on the coat and realize a simple fact. She's been collecting them on her world trip.

She's been thinking of me while she was away.

―――

ROSIE PATTERS hesitantly into the kitchen. We are only on day three, and I'm still sensing that she isn't yet fully comfortable or has made herself at home. My eyes slide into the living room where I see a tray of candles and a holder for incense on one of the living room side tables.

"Morning," she greets me shyly as I pour my protein shake into my to-go bottle.

"Hey there. I didn't wake you, did I?" I had duty yesterday and didn't see her except for a quick check-in on my way out.

She slides onto a stool and gently shakes her head. "Nah, I was up early and couldn't sleep anyhow."

"Morning sickness?"

Rosie's shoulders go slack. "A little. Not like a few weeks

ago, thankfully. I just need to eat something as soon as I wake up, I guess."

Abandoning my shake, I head to the freezer and pull out one of her oat waffles that she toasts. In my peripheral view, I notice the affection on her face, especially when I walk straight to the toaster.

"Thanks. I'll grab a drink—"

I cut her off. "Chai tea?"

"You remember?" She sounds surprised, but the faint smile of hers warms me, it's promising.

"Yeah, you used to drink it while journaling in the morning before I even woke sometimes."

Her lips press and roll in while she stays silent for a few seconds. "Carter."

My eyes flick up to link with hers. "Yeah?"

"I know the air between us since I moved in has been a little…"

"Awkward," I complete her sentence.

She grimaces. "Something like that. I just… I…" She is trying to wrap her words around a feeling, and I notice. "Give me time. To navigate living with you again. It's new but not new, and my head is a mess and my stomach a rollercoaster. It's just a lot, and it will be okay, just taking it day by day. I'll relax, already today feels better than yesterday. I hope you understand."

Her honesty doesn't scare me because it's understandable. "I get it. It's okay. I'm also tiptoeing around you, unsure what is best for this situation." *Patience.* A lot of patience.

She lets a deep breath out. It sounds as though she has been holding it in. "Good. I mean, good that we are on the same page."

I glance on the clock on the oven and decide to use it as

my escape. "I need to get a move on, as I need to be at the courthouse by ten."

"Right. Well, stay safe. Don't forget to drink your daily water."

A short laugh escapes me. "Thank you for your concern. Take it easy, call if you need anything." *Like me.*

"Of course. I'm just going to plan some classes and nap."

Our connected eyes don't seem to unwind from the knot that keeps our sight on one another. Finally, they drop, and when I leave the kitchen, I feel her gaze on me. It's heavy but feels good.

There are emotions inside her that need to unravel, and I'll wait. We have time. I just wish the clock had fewer hours.

8

CARTER

I'm slightly concerned by the amount of cheese, crackers, and fruit on the tray next to soft drinks on the coffee table in Oliver's living room.

"Did you hear me, Son?" My father, Edward Oaks, is the man that everyone in town would lay out the red carpet for. Truthfully, I'm not sure why he didn't run for mayor before he retired, but maybe he is projecting his life ambitions onto me. He's over the top with his quest for me to win, yet it's almost too humorous.

"Seriously, Carter, Deputy Sheriff Jones is ready to walk into your spot when you hang up the badge. Now, you need to ensure that you're at that end-of-summer festival in a few weeks. That's prime time to shake hands and throw on a smile for local businesses," he reiterates, because I might have let my thoughts float to other pressing issues.

My mother whispers something to Jane, the woman handling press and marketing. By that I mean she plasters a poster up here and there and tells the weekly Everhope Times what to write. The only thing earth-shattering that she has come up with is that there is a black-tie charity function next month where county and state politicians will be present, with my name even thrown around for a congressional seat one day.

"I hear you all." I give everyone a little salute.

"Good. I love your talking points. County road updates. More funding to schools. Local business incentives. What about population growth?" my brother cheekily lists, and his last comment doesn't fly by me.

I give him a warning glare. "Why are you here, again?"

"Because this is my home which I offered for your campaign headquarters since your house is for peaceful Zen only, and I wanted a snack. My wife is busy shopping with Ros—" He stops when he realizes whose name he is about to say.

It's too late. My mother's head perks up at record speed because her radar to my love life is disconcerting.

"Rose? She's here?" She begins to look around like a headless chicken. "Someone mentioned they saw her the other day, but I laughed it off that they must have been mistaken."

Right on cue, the front door opens, with Hailey and Rosie laughing, each holding a shopping bag. Their laughter fades as soon as they realize that we're not alone.

"Oliver," his wife greets him with a raised octave. "I thought you were supposed to be finished by four," she mutters under her tight smile as her eyes circle the room. By her side, Rosie's face is blank, unsure what to do.

"We ran over time. Something about free coffee for voters," he replies and awkwardly scratches the back of his neck.

"Love the communication with a warning text," she retorts.

I stand and usher myself to Rosie. "Perhaps everyone can give us a minute," I suggest.

"Why? Do you two need to talk? Maybe you should do that over dinner. Absolutely, go to dinner and talk." My mom's enthusiasm really needs to be checked by a doctor.

"*Yeah.* Dinner is probably a few steps behind," Oliver notes to himself.

Everyone privy to the details of our news whips their gaze to Oliver.

"Uh, hi, everyone." Rosie gives a little wiggle of her fingers. "I-I… was just in town to see Hailey," she lies.

I rub my face with my hands, all eyes on me.

"How about we go to the other room to talk," I recommend to Rosie.

She nods in agreement, and we quickly exit the room down the hall near the garage where Jet has been baby gated in the laundry room because my dad hates that dog.

"Shit. They weren't supposed to be here," Rosie lowers her voice and looks panicked.

I touch her arm to calm her, even though I might be having a little freakout, too. "I think we have no choice. They're never going to let me forget that you and I are in the same room right now. Plus, you said week by week, and apparently, this is our week."

Rosie fans her face with her hand. "Okay, you're right. It's not like they're my parents. You should be the one who might be having a meltdown, not me. It's your responsibility to handle this."

My lips roll in and my face strains because I'm well aware that she is right. "Fair point. I'll tell them."

"Right. You'll tell them." She doesn't sound too convinced.

"*Yep*. I'll tell them that you're pregnant." I don't seem to be moving.

She gawks at me. "Are you sure? You seem to be a little, I don't know… edgy? Could it be the sheriff in town is scared of his own parents? What a surprise." She's toying with me and feigns shock by bringing her hand to her mouth.

"You've been in my shoes, so don't even go there." My voice rises a tad in a loud whisper.

"Oh, don't you dare remind me of telling my parents before I packed a bag and left. Just tell them I'm pregnant." Her tone matches my own.

The dog whimpers, and his ears perk up as his tail wiggles. Rosie and I stall as the air seems to shift.

"Why is it quiet?" I ask. "Why do I suddenly hear nothing from the other room?"

Rosie's sight lifts to over my shoulder. "Because I think they've been listening." Her face screws up.

Of course, this is how this is going to play out.

I turn on my heel and make my way back to the room, with Rosie not far behind. She nearly runs into me when I stop as I enter the living room and my mother scurries away from the entrance, clearly having listened in. She goes to sit down then pretends to dust lint off her skirt.

You could hear a pin drop.

My father's face is resigned, and Oliver smirks to himself and tosses a cube of cheese into his mouth. Hailey and Jane just pretend to be focusing on the ceiling.

"I guess you… might… have heard." It's uneven coming out of my mouth.

"What might that be, dear?" My mother is composed yet clearly about to burst, and she never calls me dear.

A laugh bubbles deep in the back of my throat. "Rosie and I are having a baby."

My mom jumps up and claps her hands together. "This is wonderful news. The best news. You two are back together, and I'm finally going to be a grandma." She's nearly skipping to Rosie.

"We're not back together," I correct her.

Her festive demeanor is popped. "Don't be silly. Of course, you are."

My dad is suddenly rejuvenated. "Now, Carter, this is wonderful news. A great time, too. We can really angle the family man persona for the campaign. It's only fitting that you two are together if you are having a baby together. It really connects with people in our neck of the woods."

Rosie's eyes go bold just like my own; she's struggling to believe what I'm hearing.

"Oh, Edward, give it a rest… for now." My mom is holding Rosie's arms and drops her eyes to her belly. "How far along?"

"You don't need to do calculations, okay?" I intercept. I'm not going to let her count back in her head to the wedding, even if it is fucking obvious. It's her fault for dragging Rosie to that day, and it's her fault that I'm torturing myself by having Rosie sleeping in the bedroom next to mine when she should be with me.

"Wedding. My wedding," Oliver butts in, and his wife elbows him which causes him to yelp.

Another squeal from my mom, and I wish the floor would swallow me whole. "Perfect. Absolutely perfect."

Rosie is unsure how to react, but she manages to hold onto an uneasy smile.

Straightening my spine, I bite the inside of my cheek. "Okay, I think this meeting is adjourned."

"You're right. I should grab some cigars from home so we

can celebrate and talk strategy." My dad is off his fucking rocker.

I need to get us out of here as soon as possible.

I bring my fingers to the corners of my mouth and whistle to quiet the room. It works, and I even hear Jet let out a woof from down the hall. Everyone stares at me.

"Calm down. You found out. Keep your mouths shut. It's early still. Yes, Rosie is living with me. No, we're not back together, and I swear, Oliver…" I point my finger at him with a hardened look. "I could strangle you right now due to your commentary."

He grabs another cracker from the tray. "Trust me, you will do no such thing, as you're channeling your inner softer side since you're going to be dad." He winks at me, and his wife elbows him again.

In the corner of my eye, I notice Rosie's face is turning a little red. "Do you think we can get out of here? It feels a little warm."

I touch her arm and shoot daggers around the room. "Of course."

"Don't forget to grab the snack tray. I might want it later." That makes me crack a smile at least.

We walk along Everhope Road with our arms touching as we stroll and I balance the tray in one hand. We've been a little quiet, and we've walked one block.

Perhaps, it's because it's calming on the street with only the sound of a lawn mower in the distance and some kids playing ball a block up ahead. Someone checking their mailbox and saying hi. It's all the things that one would want in neighbors.

At least we no longer need to worry about who sees us together. That's a relief, but Rosie is quiet.

"You okay?" I ask.

She continues to step slowly, one foot in front of the other, and stare down at the sidewalk. "Yeah, sure... not really."

I stop and touch her arm to encourage her to face me. "What's wrong?"

"It's silly."

"No. What is it?"

She nibbles the corner of her mouth. "What?" I wonder.

"Appearances and all. Is that why you insisted that I move in?"

My eyes grow big, and my mouth opens to adjust to the silliness that just left her mouth. "Are you serious?" She nods once, and I snort a laugh in response. "Absolutely not."

The evening sun glows an orange hue on her face as she looks up and down the street. "Okay, I just thought that I would ask. I heard the words strategy, and I don't know, my head kind of connected dots that maybe it makes sense, the whole sell-the-image kind of thing."

If it wasn't for our snack necessities, then I would throw away the tray that I balance on my arm so I could touch her with both hands. Instead, I have to deal with one hand. Crooking my fingers, I scoop up her chin to lift her sparkly eyes up to chain with my own.

"It's Everhope. I'm not sure the need to sell an image is a necessity. The current mayor literally walks around in jeans and a polo. People here are just happy to have farmers' markets and clean streets. Besides, you know me better. I wouldn't do that. I *want* you to be in my house. For so many reasons, but that isn't one. It never even crossed my mind. You believe me when I say that, right?"

She nods. "Sorry. I just… my thoughts are everywhere these days."

"Mine too. You don't need to say sorry, I understand why you asked, but there is no need to. I promise," I assure her.

She now wears a tiny smile. "It's also kind of weird. I mean, do you really want to be mayor?"

"Why not?"

She snickers and steps back. "It's not your parents pressuring you or boredom? You love being sheriff, and you won't be allowed to do both."

"Yeah, but I'm ready for a change. It's less dangerous, too."

Now she giggles. "Right." The way she licks her lips, with her wry smile staying fixed, tells me she's remembering something. "I used to be scared that you would get hurt or have to answer a robbery call or something. But then you would always remind me that in this county the worse that can happen is denied permits or a hockey player speeding and trying to avoid a ticket. The only time you got hurt on the job was when a drunk guy tried to throw a bottle at a raccoon and you had to intervene. Not exactly city life. Still…"

This is the part that I always love to hear her say.

"I worry."

That's the part.

"Do you still?" I wonder.

Her mouth twitches. "I do."

That warms me still the same as it did before. "Luckily, mayor is a lot less risk. The only concern is when those city council meetings can cause a few tempers to flare."

She steps to me and reaches out to touch my shirt near my shoulder. There is no reason to, but she does. "You really want to be the guy without a badge and handcuffs?"

"Handcuffs can still stay a part of my life, just in a different way."

It causes her to blush, and as much as I'm teasing her, I'm really not.

"Fair enough. You want to listen to complaints and cut ribbon when the library has a new statue?"

"I do. I've been sheriff for many years now."

"So, you want to get your hands dirty with suggested proposals and laws and meeting minutes and all of that boring stuff before getting your picture taken because we have the state-winning pickle and you have to take a bite. And no, there is no inuendo there."

My fingers wrap around her wrist with her fingers close to me. Soft and tiny but not willing to fall because we're touching.

"In life, sometimes things change."

Like us.

"Okay then. I'll support you and not ask questions."

That causes me to smile. "That's nice to hear. Supporting me doesn't mean we need to pretend to be back together if we're not. If people don't want to vote for me because of that, then this isn't the town I want to represent."

She chuckles. "Now that is some serious political marketing right there… but you mean it."

"I do," I reply in earnest.

We stand there, not breaking contact, and I want to swipe away her wistful smile with a kiss, but I can't. We're having a baby, which is why we have to tread carefully with whatever we do.

One squeeze of her wrist and I let her go, feeling the loss as soon as her fingers drop.

"Come on, we have a snack plate ready for us to conquer." I lead us on the journey to the house.

This time, Rosie walks even closer by my side.

"You'll always be my hero with a badge." She says it so dreamingly.

This woman has always been this way. Saying things to cause people to lift their hearts. And she often hides a little bit of truth underneath the surface.

Which is why I'm waiting for the hint of what she wants.

It's better to be patient than snap and tell her how it's going to go.

My way.

9
ROSIE

I push the muffin to the side, not sure why I even bother.

"Still not feeling so great?" Hailey asks. We're sitting at a table in Foxy Rox with Esme.

I snicker as I appraise the coffee spot on Main Street. The school year just started, so Hailey is busy with the preschool she runs but managed to take some time away for an after-school break.

Foxy Rox is the best and only coffee and bakery spot around. It's trendy enough that for a moment you forget that you're in a small town. Still, one look out the window and you see the quaint center of Everhope.

"It's better. Just started my second trimester this week, and they say it lessens. So far, all indications are promising. It's just the sight of blueberries in a muffin seems to put me off. Suddenly, it sounds revolting. A shame, too."

Esme takes a sip of her latte then sets her drink down. "How is it going with sharing an abode with your ex?"

I chuckle to myself, knowing the answer is funny enough, because it could be seen as odd to many people that two ex-spouses live together. "We get along. I've been napping so much, plus driving over to Olive Owl to help plan some events for my uncles, and I'm still teaching a few yoga classes, too. Carter still has sheriff duties and his campaign for mayor. In the end, we don't see one another as much as I thought."

Hailey plays with the fork for her brownie. "Sounds like that kind of disappoints you."

"I mean, it helps us avoid major topics. Not ideal, but it makes my life easier."

Hailey smiles warily at me. "Hmm, I would say you both need to circle back to the issues."

I glance down to my belly. "You're right. I'm already getting fat."

Both women lean to their sides and look under the table before scoffing a sound. "You're really not. I can't even tell that you're with child," Esme comments.

"Yeah, I agree. Besides, it's not fat when there is a baby in there. They are two different things, so screw your logic back on your head, please."

I have a lopsided grin. "Perhaps a solid point."

Hailey smirks to herself. "I think you should take a step. Dive into discussion. He seems to want that."

"How would you know?"

Esme joins in on the wicked-look front. "Because he walked in and noticed you instantly, and now, he has this broody kind of thing happening."

I instantly steal a glance over my shoulder when I see Carter taking a cleansing breath where he's standing in his uniform, holding his hat by his side. He's always been a traditional man and never wears hats inside. He steps in our direction, unsure but also pleased by my presence.

I swing my gaze back forward and feel a flutter inside of me as if I'm a girl with a crush.

"Ladies," he greets us.

My lips roll in while my friends say hi. I feel his eyes razor into me, and I smile politely. "Hi. I didn't see you this morning."

"I didn't see you last night, either."

Esme and Hailey nearly choke on their drinks, with Hailey even needing to pat her chest.

"For the love of... Will you two get your minds out of the gutter," I chide them.

Carter's upper lip twitches, and he's keeping his entertained grin under wraps, because he doesn't seem to mind the assumed thoughts of half of Foxy Rox.

"Of course, sorry," Esme says seriously, but she can't keep a straight face.

Carter moves past the little hiccup in our conversation. "I just came in for coffee. I wasn't expecting to see you here."

"Me neither. Here." I slide my plate to him. "Have my muffin, you love blueberry."

Because I know all of his likes and dislikes in and out of the bedroom. The way he hates when I try to lead. Or the fact that he loves to pin me to a mattress. Of course, he has this whole no-shower-alone rule... when we were together, that is. And out of the bedroom, he watches hockey, hates dry grass, has an odd troll obsession, and let me once convince him to try yoga.

"Thanks." His sweltering gaze causes my clit to pulse. I'm so doomed when the extra sexually needy part hits in the second trimester. "Oh, uh, I got you some more of those candles you like. The ones that don't have a smell, just sit in those crystal healing rocks or something like that. I was out on the county road. That lady who has that store that's only open at odd times was open."

That makes everything inside of me lift with joy, and I

release a short laugh. He always thought it was crazy. When we were married, I had way too many candles all over the house, even I can admit that. "I'm sure you had a blast walking in there," I tease.

He lifts his hat up, and his brows lift then drop. "Well, she was relieved that I wasn't stopping by for law enforcement reasons, and when she saw I was clueless, she helped me out."

"I can only imagine."

"Anyhow, I should get going. Need my coffee and to head to the station."

Maybe it disappoints me a little. A low-key conversation is exactly what the doctor ordered, it seems. I don't mind a single bit. I could carry on, even if down to my toes, my body is heightened from him being close.

"Okay. See you at home," I tell him.

"Yep." He pops the P.

He rocks on his heels but doesn't move, nor do my eyes that remain latched to his, but a few seconds later, we both seem to shake away the moment.

"Ladies," he says to my friends who I forgot are here.

When he is out of earshot and across Foxy Rox to order his coffee, which is useless because before he can say anything, the barista is already handing him his black coffee with a dash of almond milk, because I got him addicted long ago.

Hailey and Esme huddle closer to the table, and their eyes blaze.

"Ooh, someone wants to do fantastic things to you," Esme whispers loudly.

"It's the eyes," Hailey adds.

"Shh. Will you quiet it down," I implore because I don't need the entire place to hear.

Esme shrugs. "What? It's obvious."

"Well, doing wicked things to one another is what got me in this position, and going into the physical-only part is a bad idea. We actually need to communicate about the bigger issues."

Hailey brings her finger to her chin to think. "Hmm, communicate. What a novel idea."

My cheeks grow big from my frustrated breath because they are relentless today… also right.

"I'm just… waiting for the right time. It's a little nerve-wracking, to be honest," I admit.

Hailey takes another bite of her brownie and tilts her head side to side. "You're eventually going to have to take the plunge. Hate to break it to you, but you also have a clock ticking."

"I'm aware." I glance down at my belly and smile softly to myself. "He or she needs parents who are not a hot mess on the relationship front, whatever it may be."

"There's a t-shirt for that, I'm sure." Esme is dead serious. "'My parents are a hot mess,'" she deadpans.

My head falls onto my arm that's been resting on the table, because that will absolutely not be a shirt that I need on the baby registry. I'm sure of it.

———

CROUCHING DOWN, I smell the rosemary that's growing in a few pots outside on the back patio. I've noticed it already, but today on this sunny day, it's extra… significant, maybe?

It's my favorite of herbs. Great for recipes, a wonderful smell, and it carries part of my name. I always had a few pots when I was married. Along with basil, lavender, and chives. But Carter only has rosemary. I doubt he uses it too. A little crack inside of me slowly seals together because these plants are not new. You can tell by the pots that he has had these for a long time. Which perhaps means that maybe, just maybe, it's because he was thinking of me.

"You noticed." The sound of Carter's thin voice causes me to flinch because he startles me.

I stand up as my body cools off from the surprise. "Geez. Scare me, why don't ya. I had no clue you were home."

That smirk crawls on his lips, with his stubble short enough today that it highlights his defined jaw. "Already for a few minutes."

My head retreats slightly. "You've been watching me?"

"Nah. Only thirty seconds, if that counts as watching."

My eyes float over my shoulder to the pots. "You have rosemary. Why?"

His tongue slides across his upper teeth, and a silence stretches for a few beats. "Why do you have a box of trolls in your room?" he counters, and yet again, my body surges with nerves.

I didn't realize he found it. There is no time like the present to be honest. I grow shy and look off to the side. "Because I collected them."

He steps closer, and my breath grows heavy. "Why?"

"I-I… just… It made me… You would enjoy them one day, plus… it's what people do when they think of someone." *Whoosh.* There, I said it.

His hand sweeps across my cheek to force me to stare into his eyes that are determined. The feeling of his hand cradling my face is firm yet caring.

"And I have the rosemary because I was thinking of you."

It seems we have always been on an unusual, shared wavelength, considering our history. Our admissions cause faint smiles to paint on our mouths.

"Well, okay. Is this confession probably why we decided to sleep together when drunk?" We both had a hidden desire because our heads have been twisted all along?

His face turns serious, but there is still a hint of a sly smirk. "Nah, that's because I purposely wanted to get you pregnant and had to fuck you senseless to succeed." My eyes pop out and my pussy clenches, because that thought… turns me on. A kink I didn't realize I have? Holy fuck.

He wets lips before he grins. "I'm joking."

"Oh… yeah… totally. I knew that."

Carter chuckles because now I'm acting a little odd, my pussy throbbing.

"Rosie."

The delicateness of his tone brings me back to why he is really circling his thumb on my cheek. "I've been thinking now that the shock has worn off over the baby news and you're feeling a little better that we should probably—"

"Talk," we say at the same time.

"Yeah. Now. I'm not really going to take a no, but I'll ask anyways. Let's grab dinner like we used to. Lay a few things on the table."

Or lay me *on the table.*

His thumb now runs along my cheekbone, trying to persuade me with a simple touch. But I need no persuasion.

"That's a good idea," I agree.

10
ROSIE

My face squinches as I study the containers of food on the counter from the riverboat restaurant. Carter got us takeout, and as much at it would all be delicious on a normal day, right now the smell of warm cheesy potatoes is making me want to turn my nose away.

He glowers at me. "You don't need to say anything. I can read your face right now." He slides all the food to one side of the counter away from me. "Peanut butter and jelly sandwiches it is."

My food refuge these days.

"You can still eat the food. Don't let it go to waste," I urge.

"I won't. I'll put it in the fridge and have it for lunch tomorrow. I would rather be on a united front with you." He walks around the island, straight to the bread box, and pulls out a loaf. The peanut butter jar comes out next from the cupboard, and then he grabs the jelly from the fridge. He ducks his head around the corner. "Grape, right?"

"Yeah." He's always been incredibly sweet, but tonight it

feels a little more endearing, especially as that sexy grin is fixed on his mouth.

"I'm sorry. This isn't what we had in mind for dinner. The morning sickness has been replaced with peculiar smells. PB & J have been my go-to from day one of finding out I'm pregnant."

He chuckles quietly in the back of his throat. "I know. It's why I stocked up on jars of peanut butter at the superstore off the highway."

I burst out a laugh. "What would possess you to come home with a box of twenty-five jars?"

He shrugs as he twirls bread bag open. "It seemed like a good idea at the time."

"We never have good ideas at the time," I retort.

His brows lift and his lips quirk out. "Not entirely true. We had some great ideas at one point."

I can't help but look at him fondly. "You're right." We got married, for one, until that imploded. I let the thought leave and choose to focus on the now. "Maybe sleeping together *was* a great idea. Now we're going to have an amazing kid, that I'm sure of."

"Yeah, yeah we are." The warm sentiment in his voice is a fuzzy blanket to my emotions.

I grab a strand of hair and wrap it around my finger while Carter finishes making two sandwiches then offers me the plate. "We also *don't* have great ideas, and that's why we are sitting here unsure how to act around each other," I admit.

He pauses and juts his jaw out to appraise me. He's waiting for me to finish a sentence because his demeanor is intrigued but too confident.

Squeezing my eyes closed tightly, I gather courage, but it's the only way we can break this tension. "I wish everything happened differently. I'm not sure what I envision for it all to have been, but this isn't where we should be now. I mean, waiting for some bubble to pop around us."

Carter doesn't say anything, and for a few long seconds, I believe it's because he is angry at me. I can say what I said, but it doesn't change what happened. We're still broken and in this very spot.

"Rosie, the best thing we can do right now is give one another a little forgiveness. It's the only way. Otherwise, we have no chance."

My eyes must brighten, and my chest rises due to piqued interest. "Chance?"

"Us. Parenting. Us again."

"Okay, but I also don't think we should try and be together because of a baby."

He reaches for my hand across the table. "He or she will always be a symbol of us, and for the next few months because your belly is growing with our baby. Doesn't mean we have to use the baby as an excuse to slowly get to know one another again and see where things go."

I stand up and escape his touch, walking straight to the glass doors to outside, and I stare across the yard. "I don't understand how we would even want to see where things go. Shouldn't we be so angry at one another that there is no chance?"

Carter growls and rakes his hair with his hands. "Woman, you are really testing me, aren't you?" He hurries in my direction. "We have to bury all of that shit, that's how we do this. I have no clue what is going on in your little head, but I let you go because if you love somebody, you set them free, and if they return then it's… I don't know what the hell they say. But you're here."

His edged tone takes me off guard because it's filled with a tenacity that could knock me off my axis. "We can't just start on a blank page." Now I'm meeting him halfway in frustration.

"Fine. Then either say what the fuck you were thinking when you were away or so help me, I will fuck the thoughts out of you," he snarls.

My mouth parts but words are stuck in my throat because he is a man who isn't afraid to be bold around me. It's just, his choice of words… well, they put images in my head that won't help our situation. I would love to see him try. "You already know that I was thinking of you. I'm just… scared, okay?"

He grabs my arm. "Of what?"

"You're supposed to hate me, and you don't. I left because maybe I needed to be the best version of myself because that's what you deserve. You are the prince that women dream about, but you didn't deserve the way I left." It spills out of my mouth because my underlying thoughts finally want to surface.

He frames my face with the palms of his hands. "Then you shouldn't be scared."

"Yes, I should. You'll resent me," I whisper.

"No. I won't." He sounds almost defiant.

"*Yes*, you will."

He closes our distance, stealing my air, and I'm a little lightheaded, but it isn't from the baby. "Rosie, I'm telling you right now. Let go of everything, because trying again is worth the thought. And we're going to do this. We'll do it so damn well that when this baby gets here, it will be as though his or her parents were never apart."

I'm shocked. I didn't see our night going this way. We are diving straight into it. So many questions. I push aside the guilt that I still feel, the remorse and shame that I let go so easily, and the anger I had for him that doesn't compare. We gave up so easily.

Now, we're in this moment.

"Carter," I whisper, and I wrap my fingers around his wrists. "I hear you. I do. I'm just…" I push out a breath and debate what to say. However, I have nothing.

"Shh. We don't need to discuss this anymore tonight. I've made my point, and that's what I wanted to do."

I always have impeccable timing when to take a serious conversation and turn it upside down. I snort a laugh because I can't help but point out, "You were going to dine me and persuade me, huh?"

In a snap, he eases and his face wilts into a small proud grin. "Right after I asked you to add all of the trolls to the shelf in the living room, yes."

He makes me giggle, and that feels nice. "I'll be happy to arrange that."

Our strong smiles grow smaller. "Rosie. You have some power over me. You never left my fucking mind, and it was torment, so I'll be damned if I don't want to grab a chance to have what I've been wanting. I shouldn't beg to try, but I will." The sincerity in everything he is doing tonight weakens me.

"You don't need to beg," I promise with a rasp. "Maybe I'm just more protective of you than you are of yourself when it comes to me." He shakes his head gingerly because he must disagree.

We say nothing and just keep our eyes locked.

Until his thumb taps my lips twice, and I want to take his thumb into my mouth, but his eyes squint and his vision narrows over my shoulder. "Ah shit, Jet got into the yard."

I quickly follow his line of sight to the dog wagging his tail in the middle of the yard, with his tail up as dirt gets kicked into the air from his shoveling paws. I can't help but laugh in hysterics. This evening really is going in all directions.

Carter lets me go and opens the sliding door to shoo the dog back home. I walk to the kitchen to grab the secret jar of treats and return to Carter. "Here. You know these will only make him return since he knows he has you wrapped around his little paw."

He yanks the jar from my hand and grumbles a sound before throwing a treat long-distance into a neighbor's yard. "Well, now the Wilkinsons can deal with him. I'll send Oliver a text."

Carter does just that, and I sit at the counter to nibble on my sandwich. "This is the world's best sandwich. You give it extra magic."

His brows furrow. "Was that supposed to be a cheesy line?"

I drop the sandwich and laugh with a full mouth. "No. Seriously, you have the right ratio of peanut butter to jelly, and it's whole wheat bread."

He clucks his tongue and proudly smirks. "I have skills." Carter takes a big bite of his sandwich while he leans over the counter. "You've mentioned a few times all the places you've seen while you were away. Did it fill your quota? Was it what you hoped?"

"No," I answer bluntly and surprise myself how quickly that came out. It was spent missing him, and I carried my heavy choices in my backpack. He stands at attention and seems perplexed by my response. "Look, you said we can kind of have a blank slate, so let's do that. We can remember the good parts and that's that."

Thankfully, he doesn't press. "Okay, the good parts. There were many."

"I agree."

"You've always been a little eccentric and unpredictable but in a good way most of the time."

I give him a pointed look. "Someone had to not be grumpy. Besides, you're... Underneath it all, you have a free spirit, too. It's just that it only seems to come out when you're with someone."

He doesn't reply, and that's fine. We both grasp that someone was me and should always be me.

"I'm going to put this food away. Want anything?"

I shake my head. "Nah. You do kitchen duty, and I will let the trolls get settled in their new home right next to the white-musk candle."

He chuckles and begins to move plates. "I'm slightly scared for your birth plan."

"Me too. I haven't thought about it too much, but we're going natural."

"You do you."

"You might not be saying that when I'm ripping your arm off from pain."

He only smiles to himself, and we both focus on our own tasks. Twenty minutes later, dishes are cleared, and the living room shelf appears a little less bare. Still, something is missing from this evening, and I'm afraid to admit what it is.

For the next hour we talk about the latest in Everhope and my family. A bit about some of the countries that I visited and some of the stories from his job that I missed. I swoon when he said that as mayor, he will ensure there is another playground in town, with a wading pool for little kids.

Basically, the nerves that I had at the start of the night are no more. This is exactly what we both needed to take a step forward.

It's when we are upstairs after turning off the downstairs

lights for the night that I realize we aren't taking just a step forward, we might be taking two.

But I don't say anything. We nod to one another good night and go our separate ways. Except, after I brush my teeth and throw on an old t-shirt, I realize that sleeping alone causes that soaring level of loneliness, and I hear thunder in the distance. A storm is coming. They always make me feel uneasy. We had a lot of tornadoes growing up.

I sigh and stare at the bed. Clicking my tongue a few times, I debate.

Then give up.

Pivoting, I slowly walk to the door of Carter's room. He left it open.

And he's lying in bed with his upper body against the headboard. Maybe he was waiting.

Still, I knock on the door frame.

"Still hate storms, huh." His voice scrapes.

Our eyes spear into one another while I twist the end of my shirt around my fingers.

"Is that why…"

"I'm not sleeping and waiting for you? Yeah."

My protector.

That's the way I've always seen him. "Do you think… maybe… can I—?"

The faintest line of victory draws on his lips.

He pats the mattress next to him. "Sleep here for the night? Because you don't want to be alone. Come on."

I smile and join him on the bed. My body imprints into the mattress, molding into the sheets instantly, as though the bed were ready for me.

But it's his arm looping around me without asking and pulling me close until I rest my head against his chest that really is the perfect fit.

11

ROSIE

Tossing my yoga mat into my basket in the corner of the living room, I stand and thrum my fingers against my side as I survey the area. I'm debating if there is something to clean or if I should just light some candles, grab a mug of tea, and cuddle with a blanket on the sofa.

I'm just edgy. Nervous energy. It makes zero sense. I can't even think of a reason why.

There is no more slew of questions about last night. Sleeping in Carter's arms felt like home, if I'm honest. I woke in the middle of the night, and I couldn't help but watch him sleep. Noticing how his arm would shift if I moved the slightest or the way his chest rises when he breathes steadily. Or the fact that his scent drowns me, between his body and steeped in the pillows. I didn't want to change clothes this morning.

I had to slip out of bed early because I had a class to teach over in Lake Spark. He should be home soon, as for the most part, he has the day shifts.

Ditching the tea idea, I flop onto the couch and decide to

call Bella. She's been hounding me with texts that I keep forgetting to answer. I've been occupied with things.

I unlock my phone and press her name. It doesn't take long for her to answer the video call. She seems to be in the corner of an office.

"Can't talk long. They have me working on a project." She quickly eyes the area. "It's a pain in the ass that I had to sign that no-fraternizing clause, because some of the players that walk into this building have me seriously doubting my life choices."

I snort a laugh. "You've always been such a by-the-book girlie. Go on, break the rules," I encourage her playfully.

She gawks at me. "Anyhow. How is it going?"

"Good. I was teaching a class this morning and now I'm going to take it easy. Actually, I'm kind of hungry. For a normal meal, finally." I note that we have leftovers in the fridge from yesterday.

"That's great to hear. And how is it with… the ex-husband?" She grimaces.

"Carter and I are fine. Baby steps, I guess. A better direction than a week ago. We had a good conversation."

My sister smiles brightly. "I'm happy to hear that. I'm really rooting for you two. I think everyone is. It wasn't a messy divorce."

I bite the inside of my cheek. "No, it wasn't. It was just a bruising blow that we both gave up so easily."

Bella shrugs. "Bruises heal."

I snicker at her. "You're supposed to be my baby sister and I'm the one handing out the deep thoughts, not the other way around."

"You told me once that bruises heal. Remember? When I broke up with my high school boyfriend."

"Nah, I believe I said he was an ass. Not quite the same thing," I remind her.

She shakes her head. "You did, but then you told me that I will heal and have a new chance for someone else."

"I don't want someone else." I toss a throw pillow to the side.

Her cheeky look annoys me. "All the more reason that it will be okay. You have him."

My heart pinches from the reality of it. Positive truth is heartwarming. "Anyhow, I'll let you go. I know you're busy with hockey players that you can't flirt with."

"Thanks." She doesn't sound enthused. "Oh, and Mom keeps mentioning that when you are further along, she's hosting the baby shower."

Now I have to laugh. "Good luck with that. I have a sixth sense that Carter's mom will blow a gasket over that. I vaguely heard planning about a balloon wall or something when Carter was on the phone with her and trying to get her to simmer down."

"You're providing all of us with entertainment. Thanks."

I shake my head ruefully, end the call, and then toss the phone to the end of the couch. I massage my neck and feel the need to stretch. I pull my leg close then hold the bottom of my foot before stretching straight out and high, nearly to my head.

"What the fuck." Carter's fumed tone causes my leg to instantly drop, and he must see that I'm confused as my gaze darts to him. Not because he must have arrived home and I didn't notice, but because he appears agitated. "What are you doing?"

"Uh… stretching." It's obvious.

He moseys into the living room from where he was standing, grabbing the throw pillow on the ground in the process. "You're pregnant. Take it easy."

I roll my eyes, aware of where this conversation is going. "I taught a class this morning if you're really in the mood to be annoyed."

He lifts his nose with eyes unwavering. He isn't impressed with me provoking him. "The class where you balance on your arms or bend like some mystical creature?"

My mouth gapes open. I'm not pissed off, more enjoying his protective side. "It's not new. I've been doing it for years. I'm careful and it's my job, so get a grip."

Carter joins me on the sofa. "Rosie, I'm serious."

I shove his arm, still completely unfazed by his concerns. "Settle down. I'll stop teaching when I feel I can't do it anymore. At home, I'm not going to stop, though. The movements will help when I deliver the baby."

His eyes blaze at me. "You are not going to deliver our baby while you balance on your head."

Giggling, I pull his arm to me to calm him down. "Relax. I promise it's fine. Now tell me, how was your day?"

He loosens up. "Fine. Just had to check a few things at the station. Nothing riveting."

"Well, that's okay. You have enough excitement in your personal life to keep your dosage full."

His cheeks tighten, and I can tell that he agrees and wants to smile like me.

"I should go change."

I nod. "Sure. I'm ready to eat a solid meal. I'll warm up the leftovers."

The back of his hand glides down my cheek. "Good to hear. I'll be back down soon."

My smile hurts.

Music was on low, a mood candle lit, and we ate dinner together. Conversation was about his brother, the latest neighborhood gossip, and going over the baby growth chart on our apps. It was casual and almost felt as though we've reached a new normal on the living situation.

And just like last night, after closing up the house, we ascend the stairs. Except this time, the moment that my feet hit the hallway floor at the top of the stairs behind Carter, he grips my hips and half turns me just enough to lift me up, and my legs wrap around his waist to stay steady.

"Here's the thing, Rosie."

Arousal zips through my body the moment our eyes meet. "Forget that you have a bed in the other room. There is only one bed that you'll be sleeping in here in this house, and it's *my* bed."

My breath catches because his hardened look won't accept any answer but yes. Power looks good on him, it always has. A bolt of lightning strikes through me and everything electrifies. It's physical and emotional, completely not going slow, but our bodies already sent us down this path a few months ago, if we're honest. The truth was lingering underneath the surface all along.

"Do you understand?" he grits out, and his eyes take possession of me.

My heart grows, and between my legs is begging for me to be under him. I'm in his trance again, and I accept that.

"Yes," I answer in a hushed tone.

"Good, you listen. Because I would lose my damn mind if you were in my bed one more time and I couldn't do this." He slams his lips onto mine.

An explosion of pent-up tension. A reunion of lips that

only know how to gravitate to one another. A confirmation that the last few days are right.

I respond eagerly by kissing him back, and his punishing lips take over as he begins to walk us into his room, still carrying me. We slow for one kiss, only for our tongues to get reacquainted. The tip of our tongues flick one another before his swirls around my own. Our lips seal just as he begins to lay me down on my back, a contrast to his damaging kisses, but then I shove him to the side and agonizingly come up to sitting.

"Wow. That was some kiss," I gasp and touch my lips.

He stares at me blankly, wondering why I pushed him away, and it causes me to smile and grab his wrists, giving him a little tug while he towers over me.

"Carter, we probably should slow it down a notch."

"How did I know that was what you were about to say?"

I shrug. "Probably because you know it too."

He sighs and looks away before swinging his gaze back to me with a pained smile. "You might be right."

"So we can start with a kiss and cuddling and see where we go?"

His boyish grin emerges. "Fine."

I pat the bed next to me. "Good. Now we can sleep with clear boundaries, and if you feel so obliged, maybe I can wear one of your shirts?"

His brows rise. "Really? You want to submit me to the torture of seeing you in my shirt?"

"I don't consider it torture. I consider it a fact that my body is beginning to feel a little different, and I want to be comfortable," I explain.

He rubs his face, trying to gather composure. "Reminding me that my baby is growing inside your belly isn't helping the situation."

I have to laugh. "It could be worse, and I could tell you that I'm willing to use your handcuffs if it means you will behave."

Carter groans and spins on his feet to walk to the drawer. "You are for sure getting a warning for disorderly conduct." He pulls out a shirt and tosses it to me.

We take a few minutes to get ready for bed, and when we both snuggle under the covers and lie on our sides to look at one another, I don't think we have any plans to go to sleep.

My gaze can't seem to drift away as a memory takes over.

He looks at me peculiarly and grimaces. "You okay there? Seem a little lost."

"Sorry. I was just remembering when we first met."

"Ah. A walk down memory lane is where we are heading."

I flop onto my back and can't seem to let it go. "It's a nice memory."

He follows suit and his back plants onto the mattress. "You were walking along Main Street in Lake Spark and paused when I was writing a ticket because someone parked outside the lines."

Snorting a laugh, I'm well aware where this is going. "I paused on the sidewalk because I wasn't impressed, and it wasn't even my car."

"You decided to voice your thoughts and told me that I must be having a shitty day if that was my concern, then pointed out a teenager down the street had littered in case I felt the need to take my grumpy mood elsewhere."

"You should have been so insulted by me, but instead, you just stood frozen in disbelief at my candor."

My cheek rests against the pillow so I can watch his facial expressions which are nuanced. "I didn't freeze because of your views. *You* took me off guard because of the way you grinned, and the flower in your hair drew me to your eyes."

A firmness presses into my heart. "Funny that I think my entire body sank when you looked up at me. Because I didn't realize how handsome you were."

"Is that why you were insistent that you buy me a coffee?" He licks his lips and smiles.

"I could tell that you needed to loosen a bolt or something. It was a beautiful day and there you were writing miserable sheets of doom for people."

He scoffs a chuckle. "So you bought me a coffee with almond milk and a cinnamon stick without even asking if that was what I drank. You said almond milk has more antioxidants and that I seemed like someone whose muscles told you that I care about my body."

I poke him with my finger. "You are making it sound like I was coming on to you using compliments." He squints his eyes at me. "Okay. Maybe I was, and it was successful because you took me for a picnic the next day. The rest is history."

We both stall, and I feel right away that maybe I didn't use the right words. History can't be rewritten.

Pulling the blanket up closer to my chin, I do a cowardly thing. "Uhm, I should probably sleep." He doesn't say anything, only reaches to the side to turn the light off. The air feels tense, and I'm aware it's my doing. "I'm sorry. I wish I had been more aware of where we each were in life then."

His hand interlaces with mine on top of the blanket. "Me too, me too… but for once in my life, you taught me to live in the moment, and that was new and exciting and good. Reality just played a game with us in the end."

"Our reality now is that we're going to be parents."

He squeezes my hand. "No, Rosie, our reality has finally

made it clear that in this moment we are where we are supposed to be."

I needed to hear that, and I'm quick to lift my body so I can kiss him firmly on the lips which he gladly accepts, his free hand gliding up my arm to cup my cheek. "Night, Carter," I whisper.

"Night, Rosie." We both shift until he is spooning me from behind.

And I sleep deeply because everything feels safe between us.

12
ROSIE

Glancing over my book, I'm slightly concerned the dog is possessed. He has been sitting in front of me with his tongue hanging out for a solid twenty minutes while I sat outside on the porch reading a pregnancy book.

"Don't you have somewhere to be, Jet?" I ask as if he will respond. Shaking my head, I'm aware he's here because he wanders and comes direct to the source of treats. Returning to my book, I continue to read about using a rebozo blanket for labor. "Apparently, it helps with gravity and pressure," I say aloud, as though he is a human companion.

The last few days have been nothing unusual except for a flood of emotions and constant thoughts about my ex-husband. Truthfully, I never want to use that title again, but I should be responsible for once and take things slow.

My phone vibrates on the table, and I grab it to see that it's my mom. Swiping the screen, I answer. "Hi."

"Hey, I just wanted to check in since it's been a few days since we last talked. Everything good with the baby?"

I snicker humorously. "Forever forward, the state of your

grandchild will be priority, huh? In my stomach, and later, out of my stomach. If this kid so much as spits up on my shirt, you'll want to know and will smile like it's the best thing ever."

"No…" I can hear her smile.

"Yeah, yeah, yeah. How is everyone?"

"Good. You know, the Blisswoods are getting ready for pumpkin season then tree season. One of your cousins started dating one of the new guys working at Olive Owl, and your uncle Knox is going to need a while to calm down."

I wince. "Eek. I'm relieved Carter was never submitted to the Blisswood interrogation tactics."

She chuckles. "It's entertaining. Also, there is a farm in the county over who had a new colt born and asked if Olive Owl has interest. I know you won't be riding a horse anytime soon, but since Astro passed, I thought I would ask."

Having a horse growing up was something that my aunt Lucy taught me to enjoy, and when my childhood horse passed not too long ago, I was sad. Astro lived on Olive Owl, but I would see him as much as I could.

"What would I do with a horse right now?"

"Maybe your child will want a horse?"

I sputter a laugh. "Uh, I think my child is first a baby and then a toddler and then maybe the age for a horse. So the answer is no."

"I thought so but wanted to check. Also…"

The line goes quiet.

"Yes?" I encourage.

"Wanted to check you are okay today, considering… the date."

I think for a second, but then it doesn't take me long, and my entire body goes rigid, causing Jet's ears to perk. I've been burying it down all day. "Ah, you mean the date I got married, so technically my anniversary if I didn't implode my life and get a divorce?"

"That." I can hear in her voice a tad of concern.

I'm not sure why it hasn't taken over my thoughts today. Did I subconsciously try to save myself from a day of misery? But now it will be all I can think of.

"I'll be fine," I answer sharply to move us along.

"Okay, if you say so. Just wanted... I'm your mom, I'll always be concerned."

Inhaling a long breath, I'm aware of her heart's intentions. "How about I come over for lunch later in the week?"

"Sure. Bear Brew like old times?" That coffeehouse is the best in Bluetop.

"They do have a good hummus wrap."

We round off our call, and I decide to return inside. Jet attempts to follow me, but I turn to him and point my finger. "You can go back to your mom and dad. You already got your milk bone from me earlier, and I know you've conned about three other neighbors on this street for more treats."

He whines but then happily runs away, which reminds me that I should point out to Carter that he purposely has never closed the hole under the fence because I know he loves the dog.

For the next few hours, I'm not able to calm down, and my walk on Everhope Road made it worse because I saw the newlyweds who bought the house up the street moving in as they unloaded their boxes from the car. They seem to be in complete bliss, and that's just a reminder of better times in my life. It also made me far too envious.

In the kitchen, I search for something to nibble on to calm my nerves, and when I spot some pretzels, I open the bag and take a bite.

"Rosie."

I'm startled and almost hit my head on the pantry door when I hear Carter. "Oh, hey, I didn't know you were home."

He strides my way with a swagger that I remember. "Just got here."

Wiping a pretzel crumb from my mouth with the back of my hand, I feel my heart quicken because I'm wondering if he realizes the date, but I'll just jump right in. "I know. Today would have been our wedding anniversary and here we are not actually married but having a baby, and I'm here and you're standing there, and you shouldn't celebrate an anniversary that doesn't technically exist anymore, but I can't erase the date." I talk at the speed of light.

Carter bites his bottom lip while he attempts to unravel my words. "Ah, so you've been occupied with the thought, too."

Sighing, I relax a tad and walk a few steps to the island to rest my forearms on. "Yeah."

The air warms when I feel him stand behind me and place his palm on my lower back. "I have no fucking clue either. We either ignore it or… it was the celebration of when we were married, that chapter, you know, but now… maybe I'm still feeling something, that I got to call you my wife and we were married on this date."

Swirling around, I didn't realize just how close our bodies are, and it's intoxicating. "It was a quickie spur-of-the-moment kind of wedding, but it was a day I'll always remember and will be a story for our child one day, right?"

"Agreed."

"We can… have a nice dinner? Maybe make that rice dish that you are talented at?"

His fingertips drop to my waist. "Sure. Whatever you want."

"Yep, a nice dinner because today isn't a normal day in a way," I repeat.

"Well, if you insist that we have an intimate not exactly celebrating our wedding dinner, then I should probably tell you that I have your favorite cherry pie in my car because I thought what the hell, today deserves dessert."

Our eyes lock for a second before we both burst out laughing, and I only calm when he swoops his mouth down to brush my forehead before dropping to catch tip of my nose, and my mouth scoops up to meet his lips for a kiss.

"Looks like we will navigate this bizarre day together then," I whisper.

His suave half-smirk informs me that I'm already in trouble. I'm trying not to remember my wedding night or how I'm sharing a bed with him again. When Carter leaves to grab the pie from his car, I stretch my arms over my head and feel weakness take over me.

Not physically but pure resolve.

"It's nice to see you eating okay." I realize that Carter has been watching me for a long time as I scarf down his cardamom rice as we sit at the island. It's a fantastic Middle Eastern dish that he's always made from a recipe book.

Setting my fork down, I decide that I'm finished. "Well, my energy is back, and I'm eating for two. Now tell me where the pie is," I joke.

He rubs my back as we are sitting next to each other. "When do you think we will start feeling him or her kick?"

"Sooner than later, I guess." I smile warmly.

He slides off the chair and gathers the plates. I would offer to help, but he will never hear of it. "Go relax on the couch, maybe pick a movie, or is it gratitude card reading time?" he teases. I always used to read one with my morning tea. Lately, I've forgotten, to be honest.

Shaking my head with a smile, I head to the couch, and a few minutes later, he joins me and I'm holding my deck of gratitude cards in hand, purely to mess with him.

Carter rests his feet on the coffee table and leans back on the couch. Him in jeans and a white tee does things to me, probably because it's criminal the way he looks and the things I want to do to him in my head.

"Surprise me."

I narrow my gaze at him while I feel my lips thin into a smile, and I shuffle the cards, before ceremonially pulling a card out. Flipping the card, my breath gets caught after I read the words.

"And?"

I hand him the card. "Be thankful now and you'll end up having more."

He drops the card, and his jaw flexes side to side. "That's telling," he comments mundanely. "Shall we discuss how the universe is conspiring?" I do see a smile he is struggling to contain.

I toss the deck of cards onto the coffee table. "It is… uh… fitting." My long finger darts out, and I feather his hand that is resting on the couch cushion between us. "I'm thankful for the baby, which I'm sure will amaze us with how much love we can have."

His face hardens, and his eyes are no longer light. "Just the baby." It's more of a question.

"Carter…"

"I agree about our child, but say what you think that has no connection to the baby," he challenges.

My eyes drop to his hand. "You mean us?" He doesn't

respond, but that's answer enough. "I don't know why but it's difficult to say aloud. Inside, I see it, but to share the words is scary."

His other hand hooks gently under my jaw to draw my attention back to his eyes. "Rosie, I think we're both on the same wavelength, so you might as well say it."

"Fine. The ba— whatever circumstances that have brought us together, I am thankful for, because you and I..." My heart is racing, and I'm about to jump off a cliff. "Maybe we will be more again."

His mouth dips down to kiss me. "We are aligned then." He speaks against my lips before kissing the corner of my mouth. "And it's not even a full moon," he rasps before kissing me.

I smile as my body sinks into a mood that only he can take me into. Slowly, I move, and my fingers push against his chest to make room so I can swing my leg over until I'm straddling his hips. Sitting on top of him, I feel the thickness under his jeans that presses against my middle. I loop my arms around his neck, and his hands frame my waist.

His eyes chase mine, and he is letting me lead, but our destination is straight back into our mouths melding together for a kiss.

Now it's unbearable. My body is on fire, and all the ideas I've had the last few days of taking steps no longer feel logical. I'm in this with him. It's a special day, but only because it reminds us that there is good still left in us, possibly better.

And I'm desperate for him right now.

"We shouldn't have these conversations when you are wearing your tight white shirt that shows your muscles," I coo as my mouth trails along his jawline. "It does things to me."

"I want to do things to you," he whispers.

The heat building in my body is overwhelming. Screw kissing, I need him to screw me.

But I already know that it will be more than a quick fuck. This isn't that at all. Too many emotions are involved, and we will go slow.

And I'm okay with that.

"I think we should go upstairs," I suggest in a sweltering husk.

I'm not even sure how he does it, but he manages to stand, taking me with him as my legs remain wrapped around him. I giggle, but he is now on a mission and won't get distracted.

As soon as we are upstairs and on his bed, he gently guides me to get comfortable. I didn't even realize we've already ended up here because I'm too lost.

I watch as he peels his shirt up his body, revealing his toned abs. Gosh, I'm enjoying that he stays in shape. It's an extra perk.

He's on a mission as he pulls my legs up to drag my leggings off and my panties too. It's happening so fast, and it's driving me crazy, but I need him right now, just as he wants me. The air against my pussy only increases the sensitivity around my clit. When he reaches down to work my shirt off, his warm skin grazes my middle, and my body seems to accept the scent of his aftershave.

Completely naked on the bed, with my nipples now little pebbles from the coolness in the room, I can't help but let my thighs part a little wider. Carter's gaze drops down to take in the vision of my naked body on top of his bed.

"I'm going to take in the view every single night." He lowers himself between my legs, but his gruff chin prickles my skin as he nips up my thighs and then above my pussy, stopping right below my bellybutton.

The feeling of his lips feathering my belly causes my body to arch up slightly. Right now isn't sexual, it's something else.

He places a soft kiss on my stomach. "You are so unbelievably beautiful."

"Carter," I plead, already breathless.

His tongue circles around my bellybutton before his lips travel barely above the little slope of my belly. "Even more beautiful because our baby is in here. I did this to you," he murmurs against my skin.

I peer down to see him worshipping my body, and it's poetic as much as it's passionate.

My entire body is on fire, and I'm aching in agony. Lowering my hands, I claw his soft hair that is just the right length for me to hold on to. I encourage him to move lower. Instead, he moves back up, bypassing my stomach, and his tsk vibrates against my skin, making my nipples harder.

"Rosie, we don't regret making a baby, but I regret that I didn't take my time to worship you the night we did it," he rasps.

A string that connects my heart and pussy tugs.

He latches onto one nipple, and I moan. Still his hair is between my fingers as he begins to play with the other nipple, twisting and plucking while he sucks on the other, even pulls a little with his teeth.

I whimper from how it sends a signal straight to my pussy.

"These tits. Already growing," he says against my skin.

I'm about to lose it. My knees part further, and I tilt my hips up to find friction from his jeans against my bundle of nerves. He has a devilish laugh because he notices. I attempt to push him lower by encouraging him with his head, but he won't have it.

He stops and rises to kneel. "You seem not to remember that you only listen when we're in bed. Put those arms above your head."

My breath is softly heaving from every little touch and word that he says. I obey and stretch my arms above my head, causing my body to splay in full view for him.

"Good girl." His eyes are predatory in the best possible way.

He returns to me by moving himself to the floor and between my legs that are hanging off the mattress. I can feel I'm completely soaked, and when Carter lashes his tongue against my pussy, it causes me to whimper and my hips to buck.

His tongue laps up and down a few times before finding home on my clit where he swirls and nips. I'm cursing a slew of words I don't even understand, and he moans as he licks me, with no sign of abandoning me, and plunges a finger inside me as I wail his name.

Carter's eyes flick up with a satisfied grin against my pussy. My fingers clench the duvet above my head, and I can't tear my eyes away from him between my legs.

"You're always wet for me. Always ready for my cock. A good little girl ready to be taken."

"If you don't get inside of me right now, then I'm going to…" I grit out.

That wicked chuckle returns, but it only causes me to lift my pelvis a little because I'm serving my body to this man.

But he deserts my drenched pussy and stands. The sound of the buckle clinking open is always the part that heightens the tension because I know that any second, he will be inside of me where I desperately need him.

I get my wish because his knee parts my legs, and he uses his tip against my slickness to coats his cock. Our eyes tether together as he enters me, causing us to moan in sync with one another.

"This is mine again. Do you understand?"

"Yes," I moan out.

He plunges deep into me and hard, and I wail from the sensation. I'm not in pain, but he is touching me in parts that only he can. With a grunt, he does it again.

"Tell me if it's too much. It's a little different this time…" The way he says that in a funny tone, I know he means because I'm pregnant.

"Don't stop. I'm fine."

We roll our hips together, and it's taking everything in my power not to come yet. Being sandwiched between his body and the bed is where I'm supposed to be. A prisoner of my free will.

He interlaces our fingers but doesn't let my arms fall. "Fuck, you feel good." His hot breath tickles my ear.

We slow down, and with this thrust, the magnetism of what we're doing floods our eyes. We meet halfway for a kiss. A crushing kiss of two people not just in bed for the fun of it.

"Rosie," he mutters in the tone that I remember as the side of him that is his opposite.

He's always demanding in bed, but I treat it more as a spiritual wave.

When we come together, it's a perfect fit.

"I know," I whisper. "I know." I'm completely breathless.

Another pump and then another, our rhythm picking up.

It feels so damn good to feel dizzy, and it isn't because of our baby inside of me.

It's because of the man who was once my husband.

13
CARTER

It's been a few weeks, and I'm not sure we've left this bed, but we have. Except mornings are a struggle. Just like today.

Which is more the reason that we are perfectly content here when the clock says it isn't yet seven in the morning, but there is a little light sneaking through the blinds. Rosie's in my arms as I spoon her from behind. It's become a habit that my hand rests on her belly. There's a little curve, but her belly isn't the same as even a week ago. She has a radiance about her these days.

A few years ago, she glowed brightly because she was a free spirit who had no intention to let anyone have a bad day. Now? She's still a free spirit, but now with a little more direction. Maybe it's the age gap and our maturity levels were different but we chose to ignore it, or it could simply be that Rosie had to grow into someone she might have always wanted to be.

It has been a whirlwind. Our anniversary reminder that started out as a haunting but quickly changed into a reminder of what we were and could be.

It doesn't matter how we got here in this bed but yesterday led us to it.

She's here naked in my arms and begins to stir with those blissful little noises that she makes when she wakes. Her body wiggles against mine which doesn't help my cock, but I've got to give her a minute before I slip right into her because she's always ready.

She begins to stretch and yawns as her hand falls to cover my own on her middle.

"Morning," she says groggily.

I plant a kiss on the curve of her shoulder. "Morning." I begin to trail kisses up her neck, and the hint of apple is still in her hair from her shampoo. "You just rest right here, and I'll take care of something."

She snorts a laugh. "If you mean morning sex, then I'm all on board."

I grin against her skin from her permission. Truthfully, she's been a little extra frisky, shall I say, and as much as it's me, I have to give some credit to hormones.

My finger lazily feels between her legs. Pressing against her clit a few times, I align myself and plunge right into her heat. She fits like a glove, and her hum every time I slowly rock into her only brings on my own moan.

I play with her nipples, giving them a pinch, and then give her clit a little more attention until she interlinks our fingers and rests our hands back on her belly as I continue on our quest for a release. We get there, and I fall back and sigh, as my heartrate needs to lower.

I'm in a daze, but Rosie is now fully awake and rolls to her side to look at me. She rests her head on a propped elbow, and her wistful smile doesn't fade. "Need to recover, old man?"

I bark a laugh and pull her to me so her head can rest on

my chest. "Don't start, otherwise I'm tying you up tonight to prove a point."

She giggles, and her fingers begin to trace the lines on my chest. A silence grows, and it's a sign that she's going to ask like she always does. "Are you sure we aren't screwing this up? Getting stuck in lust and not thinking about the consequences? Should we be moving slower?"

I raise a brow at her, unimpressed. "You know the answer."

Her lips pinch right before she plants a kiss on my chest. "It's okay, I'll follow you. I'm a prisoner in your bed, and there are worse things," she muses.

I squeeze her arms and keep her tight to my body. "Good girl."

"I just want us to get everything right."

I refrain from giving her the long explanation today. "We will. Not hiding from everyone is already a solid step, nor are we rushing to get a marriage license." Which hasn't exactly *not* crossed my thoughts.

The mention of marriage causes Rosie to still. I can calm her about the now, but whenever it comes up about marriage number two or the long-term living situation, she recoils. Soon we will need to start planning the baby's room, and it has to be here so she is rooted down to this house.

Because I'm a man possessed to make her mine again.

Mostly because I see it in her eyes that it's what she wants too.

Her nails thrum on my chest. "Anyhow, we have an ultrasound coming up, and we can find out if it's a girl or boy… Do you want to know?"

I can't tell if she is testing me. "It's your choice."

She rolls out of my arms to her back and stares at the ceiling, but a smile skates across her mouth as she mulls it over. "I think not. Keeps us in suspense."

Oh. I wasn't expecting that. I kind of thought we'd had enough shocks when it comes to us, but okay, she's running the show.

"Sure." My response lacks enthusiasm.

She laughs. "Convincing. How about we decide on the day?"

"Deal."

She yawns again and rubs her eyes. "Ah, the real world awaits us."

I give her a quick kiss on her cheek, sit up, and slide out of bed. Walking straight to the bathroom off my room, I turn on the shower. While the water warms, I stand at the doorway to see Rosie has grabbed her phone and is checking a message.

"Joining me in the shower?"

She snorts a laugh and gets out of bed, holding her phone up when she stands in front of me. "Our moms are losing the plot."

I do a quick skim.

Mom: Obviously, when the time is right we will have the baby shower here at Olive Owl.

Carter's Mom: Obviously, it's more appropriate to have the baby shower here in Everhope where my son and the mother of his child live.

Mom: Then all the more reason to let us host the baby shower so she can still involve all of the family.

Carter's Mom: But Olive Owl isn't that far away, so all family can come here to Everhope.

Mom: Again. Shall I remind us all of our family size? Rosie has her dad, three uncles, two aunts, two siblings, and about eight cousins, nobody knows the exact number as we all lost count. It's my little girl, so the shower will be here at Olive Owl.

Carter's Mom: And it's my little boy.

Hailey: Or… we just have the baby shower at her sister-in-law's/friend's place so none of you win. Wow, what a smart idea. Give Hailey an award.

Rosie sets her phone on the dresser. "See?"

"Damn. It's a little out of hand."

We both make our way to the shower and step under the hot water as steam fills the bathroom.

"I'm scared about what happens when they discover that we're not finding out if it's a boy or girl. Speaking of which, after the ultrasound, I'll be halfway, so we should probably start to think about what things we need. I really want to go for simple. Definitely get one of those wraps so I can carry him or her around. Obviously, we need natural baby soap and all of that stuff. We need to get an amethyst crystal to help with sleeping, and—"

I interject. "Rosie. Relax. We have time."

Her head wobbles side to side as she grabs her body wash. "Sorry. It's just the list is in my head."

I begin to lather soap on my body. "It also means we need to set up the baby's room," I casually mention.

"Maybe, the small room across the hall, right?"

I stop mid scrub, doubting if I just heard her. We've moved up the scale from a no, to a maybe on this house being where she and the baby will be staying on a more permanent basis, to a probably yes. Her eyes swim side to side because I don't think she even realized she said it.

"Was that your subconscious?"

Her mouth parts open, but only a croaky sound escapes. "Well… I guess. It makes sense, right? Actually, it doesn't matter, the baby will sleep wherever I sleep because of night feeds." Now she's sweeping what she said under the rug.

But I'll have none of that. I snake my arm around her waist to bring her flush against my body. "It's okay. I won't make a big deal about what you just said. I'm only going to highlight that you said a room here. That's something. I'm going to ask you, and you'll answer honestly. No bullshit. Then we can happily get on with our day. We even still have those fake sausages that you like with toaster waffles."

She bites her bottom lip, bracing herself. "Okay. We said we will go slow even though we're sharing a bed. Apparently, it seems that a little more may have crossed my mind, and obviously something in my head decided to share it with all of us. Does that satisfy your standards of an answer?"

I kiss her forehead. "It does. I also get to analyze it, and it would suggest that I need to move some furniture out of that room. Would you like me to do that?" I'm coaxing her to be a little more blunt and see where we are exactly on the maybe line.

The way she grumbles, with her lips doing a little pout, is freaking adorable. "Yes." It chirps out of her mouth at record speed, and it takes a few moments longer than normal, but her mood disperses, and that warm smile appears.

"Okay. Do you want me to pick up spinach when I'm at the grocery store later?" I'm keeping my word and not making a big deal about this small win.

She shoves my shoulder slightly because she understands what I'm doing, and her eyes flood with appreciation. "That would be great. I'm still trying these healthy smoothies for pregnancy."

"How's that going for ya?"

"They're revolting. Why can't I just have a chocolate shake, throw in a spoon of peanut butter, and call it protein and antioxidants? So what if I decide to throw a bucketload of whipped cream on top and a bunch of those cocktail cherries."

"Then do it. You don't need to do everything by the book, not unless it says sex helps during pregnancy, because that advice, we are going to follow without fail."

A beaming grin floods her face as she continues to wash herself. It's always kind of dangerous when I watch her clean between her legs where I marked her, because I just want to do it again now.

Alas, we do have things to do today. I have work. Rosie is off to teach a yoga class. I hate that she's driving out of town, and I'm not 100% that she should be doing all of that bending due to the pregnancy, but she assures me it's fine and reminds me that bendy is how we like it.

I trust her on it, so I let it go.

She quickly kisses my lips and begins to leave. "It's been fun, but I gotta go."

I grab her arm to stop her. "Then no way am I getting a chaste kiss."

"Forgive me, Sheriff."

Then she kisses away her mistake.

ALL WEEK ROSIE has been anxious about this appointment, but when she said that she began to feel flutters in her stomach and realized that it may be the baby, then she was all smiles again. I got nothing when I touched her, but they say that's normal.

"Everything looks great." Dr. White is still moving the probe around over Rosie's belly that has a layer of gel.

Rosie and I smile at one another as I hold her hand.

"Did you two want to find out the sex?"

"No. It's okay. We'll wait," Rosie answers calmly.

The doctor's eyes bounce to me, and she must see that I'm not 100% in agreeance, but it's Rosie's choice. Rosie notices too.

Creases appear on Rosie's glowing face. "You want to know?"

A croaky sound escapes me.

The doctor smiles ear to ear. "You're not the first parents to find yourself in this situation. Either way, I can write it on a card in an envelope and you or someone can open it when ready, or I can tell one of you and you can keep it to yourself," she explains the options.

"Who in their right mind would have one parent find out and not the other? Like, how do you not burst with that knowledge?" Rosie thinks it's a crazy idea. My lips quirk out, and I rub the back of my neck. Rosie then gawks her eyes out at me. "Are you serious? You would do it?"

I shrug. "I mean… obviously it works for some people."

Her eyes stay wide. "You know you can't hold it in. Don't we have complications enough considering you're my ex-husband and here we are with your baby inside my belly?"

Ooh, sassy.

The doctor attempts to bite back her grin when the information we all already know is said out loud. Plus, she's witnessing us quarreling, although it's hilarious.

I kiss Rosie's hand. "It could be fun."

Rosie's sight circles the room because I'm not sure she believes what she's hearing, and truthfully, I never thought of it as an option. Contrary to Rosie's beliefs, I am great at keeping secrets.

I give her fingers a little squeeze. "You always said we should follow adventures."

She studies me for a hot second before a smile begins to crack because I'm winning her over. She smacks her lips together. "Okay. Let's try this and humor him that he actually believes he can keep it to himself for the next twenty-ish weeks."

I quickly give her a peck on her lips.

"Love when couples do this." Dr. White moves the screen slightly so Rosie can't see. She indicates for me to join her by the machine, and I do.

Rosie is still shaking her head in disbelief as she stays lying down.

The doctor zooms in on the screen. "I'm going to show you, but to clarify, I will input the gender in the computer, but I won't print this one or put it in the app that we use to share with our patients."

I rub my hands together. "Okay, let's do this."

The doctor uses her finger to show me the area that she squared in on and quickly types into the keyboard.

I keep my best poker face when all I want to do is grin.

This is going to be a good story. She thinks I will let the secret escape my lips, but I know she will be begging at some point.

"Alrighty. It seems we are done and you two can go." Dr. White offers Rosie paper towel to clean her belly. "You can make an appointment at the desk for your next follow-up."

Rosie and I both say thanks, and we are left for a moment alone.

Instantly, my ex-wife waves her finger at me with a scornful smile. "You are so bad."

"And that's the way you like me."

She shakes her head and hops off the exam table. "Come on. We got through another day together, let's just call that a win."

Every day lately is feeling like a victory.

14

ROSIE

Bella squeals at me while we chat over coffee for her and tea for me at Foxy Rox. I love fall, and the October colors outside with crunchy leaves are everything the Blisswoods enjoy during pumpkin season.

"I'm going to grill Carter. You don't want to know, but I do," she reminds me.

It's been a week since we had my appointment, and so far, Carter hasn't let it slip if it's a boy or girl inside me. I can't even read him to get a hint. I still don't want to know, but I'm also happy he has something for himself. I have the whole pregnancy while he watches on.

My sister is like a little penguin with her arms flapping. "I guess you're going to do grays and light green or yellows in the baby room."

I laugh nervously to myself while my hand rests on my belly. "Throwing me the reminder that I'm setting up a nursery in Carter's house, eh?"

"Well, you two are kind of together again, right?"

I nod and grab a piece of the giant chocolate chip cookie on my plate. "We're going slow. Jumping right in and saying we'll drive off into the sunset is maybe a stretch. After all, I hurt him."

That's the whole issue. I can't seem to get past the block in my head that I shouldn't have forgiveness or if I screw up that he'll easily let me go again. I've made mistakes, and I've been trying to give myself compassion on that front. I should admit to him clearly what I have now come to realize, and it's that this baby is helping me clear my thoughts even more.

"I think you two will be fine. The way you look at one another is… special." She seems fond of my happiness. One day, she'll have it, too. I'll be the one on the other end of the table offering advice that I should probably be listening to myself right now.

"Anyhow, we're going to start to look at things for the baby. Apparently, furniture might have quite a delivery time. Plus, if I have to hear the moms beg me for a gift list one more time, I might lose it. I'm positive if this kid can hear that he or she has already learned to stop listening when it involves their grandmothers."

Bella chuckles and pulls her hair into a ponytail. "As much as it really would be great at Olive Owl, at Hailey and Oliver's is fine too." Her sentence abruptly ends, and she offers a welcoming smile to someone over my shoulder.

I glance to my side as my second cousin, Gracie, arrives with an ear-to-ear smile and dressed in a stylish skirt and coat.

"Hey, ladies, fancy seeing you here." Bella scoots over, and Gracie has a seat on the booth bench.

"You would see me more if you actually slept at your apartment here," I tease her. She has a great loft above one of the stores on Main Street. We meet for the occasional coffee, but she's busy.

She shrugs. "Sorry. My mom has kept me occupied at the

boutique, and I'm working on some designs." Her family has a lingerie boutique and label over in Lake Spark. Her dad was a professional football coach and is also the dad of my aunt's husband.

"Do you have any samples in your car? Family perks and all," Bella tries her luck.

Gracie flashes her brows at me. "Not today, but we do have a great maternity line back at the store."

I pause for a second to consider if it might be needed, considering I'm sleeping with my ex again. "Thanks," I answer simply.

"So what are you ladies talking about?" she wonders.

Bella snorts a laugh. "Rosie doesn't want to have her baby shower at Olive Owl."

Gracie's mouth opens as her entire face tightens from her amused shock. "Your dad won't like that at all. But kudos for being brave enough to deny the Blisswoods a family event."

I shrug. "I mean, it will be winter, so we'd only be inside anyway. It's still a while away. I was thinking that we could do Blessingway since we will be all women. It's a tradition, and it will be great. We'll make a bracelet from beads that I can wear during labor, and we can all light a candle." Already, I'm smiling in excitement.

Bella stares at me blankly. "Is that the ceremony you dragged me to once where you spread cacao paste on your face and go around a circle to share your inner thoughts?"

"No. This won't be a cacao ceremony, and you loved that, by the way. It cleared your skin for days."

Gracie nods. "Yeah, that was a miracle," she comments seriously.

"I don't care what we do, as long it gives me some good juju to find a guy." Bella drinks from her coffee.

I narrow my eyes at her. "You're still young. You have time."

"I guess."

I glance at my phone screen to see the time, and I have to get on with my day since I have a few errands. "I'm going to have to head out."

"No worries. I'll catch up with Gracie then head back home before Mom flips out that I'm late for dinner. It's like I'm forever ten or something."

Gathering my purse, I recall the feeling. "Leave her alone. She was always meant to be a mom. Always puts us first. It's probably why I remember so many things from when I was little, all the way back to when I was three and carried around a unicorn named Jelly everywhere."

My sister reaches out and touches my hand. "You're also meant to be a mom and are putting the baby first. That's why you seem to struggle a little with your emotions and it isn't hormonal. You just want it all to be right."

Gracie watches us with affection.

We stand and give hugs goodbye. "Sister, oh so wise you might have become."

Or just a speaker of the truth, but I'm not going to highlight that.

A WEEK LATER, I notice that there are a few questions etched on people's faces as Carter and I stroll side by side in the baby store a few towns over. It's probably because I'm next to a guy in a uniform, and if it wasn't for the fact that I'm visibly pregnant then one might assume I'm in trouble for shoplifting.

I shoot the little scanning gun at the box of diapers on the shelf.

"We've walked around the entire place once and you've only scanned a box of diapers. You know, we might need a little more than that," he teases me.

I read the screen on the scanner and notice how empty the list is. "Sorry. I want to have fun with this, but I can't help feeling guilty that people want to buy us gifts."

He snorts a laugh. "Because they want to. They're all still battling it out who will throw a baby shower that is way over the top, too."

Shrugging, I glance at the baby wipes. "I know, but when I was traveling, I saw so many mothers who all they had was their baby, worn-out clothes, and maybe a wrap to hold them. They had nothing, and here I am about to scan away."

Maybe it's because I just reminded us that I disappeared across the world which causes Carter to halt and draw in a breath, but his gleeful attitude for today seems to vanish. He touches my elbows, his eyes clouded with insistence.

"Rosie, you have a good heart. You didn't need to travel the world to figure that out."

It cuts through me because it means I didn't need to leave at all. My lip begins to tremble because it's yet another blow to being aware of my mistakes.

Carter realizes that his words were a little harsh, even though his tone is anything but. "Forget I said that." He glances away.

I sniffle. "No. It's okay. You meant it and are probably right."

"I am right." His finger catches my chin to guide me back to his warm eyes. "You have a good heart is what I mean. I already know that whatever we get that you don't need, you will donate somewhere. You don't need to feel guilty or selfish. You're allowed to enjoy this. I want to enjoy this… with you."

I'm beginning to find tranquility again, and his smile calms me. He seems to have the power to chisel away a little worry inside of me.

"Stop feeling like everything you do is wrong. You're going to be a great mom and need to worry less."

"Bella said the same." I press my lips together.

Carter steps forward and brushes a soft kiss on my forehead. "It's because sometimes it's others who see it before we do."

He plants another kiss on the tip of my nose, and my body now feels fully relaxed. Also, because I brush away my own self-doubt that one day our past will come back to bite us.

"That's it." He yanks the scanner out of my hand and tugs my arm to keep us moving. "What kind of crib are we searching for?" Carter is getting us back on track.

"I'm not sure. My uncles mentioned they might build one. Will we need pink or blue blankets?" I slip that in to test him.

He smirks at me. "I'm not sure." He thwarted my attempt to break him.

Something else flickers inside me, and I can't keep it in. Another strike of silence falls upon us when I pull on his arm to stop him on his quest. "Carter…" He stares at me and waits. "What you said earlier about not needing to travel the world to figure out that I'm a good person… I think I realized that the world is big and I'm just a tiny speck on the map, but…" I inhale a sharp breath. "I only want to be that small speck on a map with you."

He steps forward and combs his hands through my hair to cradle my head with that familiar glint in his eyes. "I'm happy you realized." He kisses the top of my head. It's a little while of us standing in an embrace in the middle of the store before he breaks our sentimental moment and moves me forward. "Now, let's continue with what we were supposed to do today. Go around this store as parents to our kid."

I pinch his arm as we turn down the aisle. When I see a basket of the cream and shampoo that I want, I point for him to scan. Then there is the bouncy seat I see up ahead, and there are blankets in the distance. The next hour is fun, and I needed to laugh, it's cleansing for the soul.

Walking between the hanging clothes, I can tell Carter is toying with me. With his coy smile, we walked around the girl section which causes my brows to rise, only for him to then walk us through the boy section. Finally, he settles on the clothes that can be for either and scans away. Mostly, white onesies. He's not going to falter.

———

BY THE TIME we're finished and have picked up lunch from the drive-thru on the way home, I concede that I'm in a good mood.

Walking into the house, I stop at the bottom of the staircase and decide that I need to change. Clothes are fitting a little differently these days.

"I'm going to steal one of your button-up shirts from your closet. I'm running out of clothing options while the kid morphs inside my body. I'm going to order a few things online later," I say, and I'm already on the first step before Carter can answer.

He pats my ass. "Stealing might get you put in jail, Rosie." His voice is full of sweltering innuendo.

"I might be on board with that."

Carter follows me because he needs to get out of his uniform, and we'll just have an easy night in.

When I'm halfway inside the walk-in closet, I'm already peeling off my long-sleeve shirt to leave me in my black bra. I can hear Carter opening a drawer in the other room. My eyes search for a shirt. Buttons allow me to loosen where needed, plus the smell of Carter getting soaked into my skin isn't a bad thing either.

I spot a light blue one and pull it off the hanger, only to notice a shoebox with a lid ajar on the shelf behind. It draws my attention a little longer because it seems to be empty except for a few things.

The feeling of arms snaking around my middle and over my bump surprises me. "No you don't." Carter nuzzles his mouth into my neck. He is down to his white undershirt that always highlights his arm muscles.

I smile. "Why not?"

"Did you find a shirt?"

He's brushing past my question. "Uh, yeah."

"Good. We should go find a movie to watch."

I twirl around in his arms, smiling because now I'm even more intrigued. "You didn't answer my question."

"Nothing."

I squint and study his eyes that seem nervous.

Ignoring him, I turn and reach for the box and pick it up to check inside. Suddenly, I know why he didn't want me to find it.

My fingers wrap around the circular rings in the bottom of the box, and I slowly hold them up, letting the shoebox fall.

A giant wave of emotion takes over my body. My throat runs dry as my eyes drill into my palm that's holding two rings. One that was his and the one I gave back, even though I wanted to keep it to remember our chapter, but I didn't, because it made it easier for me to leave.

I can hear Carter sigh behind me while I get entranced at the view.

"You kept our wedding rings?" I gasp softly. I shift to face him, and his lips are rolled in as he's pinching the bridge of his nose.

"What was I supposed to do? Throw them into the river?"

"I-I…" Have no words.

He snatches the rings from my hand only to curl his fingers over them as if he can still hide what's already been undone.

"We both have hidden things that we've kept. Mine is just a little more profound than a scary-looking troll from Norway."

"Which will not be finding a shelf in the baby's room," I say blankly.

The line of his mouth tugs. "We've both been scorned by one another, but we kept little parts so we wouldn't forget the good moments."

"They were not just good but perfect," I correct him sadly.

I lift my hand to set it on his chest, and his free palm covers my own near his heart. "We're on the right path, Rosie."

"I'm slowly beginning to see that. Healing can't always be fast."

A pounding nudge hits the wall of my stomach, and I flinch, instantly bringing both hands to cradle my belly. It breaks our moment.

"Are you okay?" Alarm is in his voice.

But I just let out a laugh with my beaming smile. "Very." I giggle. "Our baby has a thing for interrupting us during crucial conversations, it seems." I capture Carter's hand and place it on the side of my stomach. "I'm positive that you'll feel this finally."

His hand stills, and his face quickly spreads into the brightest smile I've seen as he feels the baby kick. "That's the baby?'

"No, it's a dinosaur," I deadpan before smiling brightly. "Yep, it's the baby." My gaze drops down to see our hands together. "Our baby who has a thing for timing when their mom is in a bra and their dad is holding our old wedding rings."

Carter grins. "Clearly he or she is an agreement of something or simply wants to lighten the mood."

Our eyes meet, and it's the best warm and fuzzy feeling of the day. The baby has timing for sure.

From the moment he or she was conceived, actually. A pure mission to bring together two people, and today they are just reminding us of their scheme.

Another sharp kick flutters against the wall of my stomach. "Or perhaps... just reminding us that there are better moments ahead."

He kisses my forehead again. "I put this baby inside of you, and they're strong."

"Tell me about it. The other night, I woke and its tiny feet were shuffling inside of me. But it's the best pitter-patter."

"Rosie..."

I lean my head forward to rest against his chin, aware of the question he wants to ask. He doesn't need to, I answer anyway. "We're not anywhere near rings, but... they don't need to go anywhere. Just don't pressure me about it. But you don't need to hide the rings anymore."

"Deal."

We crack a smile at each other before another jab causes our attention to shoot down.

"Seriously, this kid added to a touching moment, but now it just kind of hurts," I complain.

Carter begins to rub circles on my belly. "Give the baby a moment and I'm sure they will get the hint to calm it down."

And the baby does get the clue because the kicks fade away. Carter takes the box and places it in the top of his dresser while I button the shirt.

His speed to undress to his boxer briefs impresses even me. His hunting eyes trap me, and a few swaggering saunters is all it takes before he is on his knees in front of me. The shirt on me doesn't deter him, and his hands are already climbing up my legs as he plants a firm kiss against my belly.

"You're so incredibly beautiful."

"You've mentioned once or twice," I relay.

He bypasses my humor, and he hooks his fingers under my panties and pulls them down my legs. His eyes rocket up to my face, and the lust in his eyes is overbearing. I feel it between my legs.

His hands sneak under the shirt, with his palms facing up above my waistline, but his mouth hovers lower, sending a ripple from my clit up my body to my sensitive nipples. The wide-open kiss over my pussy only multiplies the sensation.

When Carter stands, his fingers play with my pussy while he kisses my mouth slowly to ensure I taste myself.

I moan from the pure sensuality of it all.

He leads our direction because I'm unable to see. His mouth is a force on my lips demanding I kiss him back, and I want to.

He needs to be inside me because this man consumes me in every way.

The back of my knees bumps where the ends of the duvet and mattress meet, and as much as he would push me until I'm on my back, I've heard it suggested I should be on my side, on top of him, or on all fours. It's better for the baby they say, and I'm not going to argue as long as I get to continue to have Carter inside of me.

He decides our position of choice, and I straddle him while he sits up in the middle of the bed, and I loop my arms around his neck. We don't need to say anything because the last few minutes have said it all. There are rings in the room, and a child that is ours.

Reality has set in that we're moving along our road.

I plunge down on top of his hard cock and coo from his length pistoling straight up inside of me. He keeps my face firmly in his hands, caging me in while our mouths fuse together and I rock on top of him.

When we're not connected by our lips, our eyes are staking one another in agreement that this is where we are.

Together.

15

CARTER

I shake Betsy's hand, the woman who owns the dry cleaner. I've just finished hearing her talk about her worries that we still have parking meters on the street, even though they are no longer in use. They confuse people, she says, and I have to agree. I can now add that as a campaign issue.

However, as I let her hand go to move on to the next person on this busy occasion in Everhope, I can't help but notice that Rosie's dad is standing across the square where Christmas tree lights were just lit. He's been staring at me with a fierce look for a few minutes.

"Uh, Rosie," I interrupt her saying hi to someone, as she's stayed close to me for the last thirty minutes.

"Yes, Future Mayor?" She's been in a good mood all day and for the last few weeks, with an added dose of bubbliness.

"Why is your father not exactly in a festive spirit?"

She interlinks our arms covered in thick coats, with the cold air hitting our noses. "Because he is still a little pissed that we didn't join them at Olive Owl yesterday for Thanksgiving." There is zero concern in her voice.

We opted to skip her family dinner because it's a chaotic mess with way too many people, plus two dogs. The chickens can get a little vicious, too. Her aunts drinking family wine? Things get crazy.

Instead, we opted for a quieter day at my brother's with just a few friends. We were there for a few hours then went straight home for sleep.

I thought inviting Brooke and Grayson for cider on the square was a good idea.

"Okay, but do we need to spike his cider or something? He seems a little tense."

She swats my arm. "Relax. He's messing with you." To prove her point, she drags me with her to her parents. Her mom is all smiles and enjoying a piece of pie from the stall nearby, and her father finally breaks and offers a faint smirk.

"How is it going? I know the cider isn't the same as at Olive Owl, but it's close enough." Rosie gets our conversation moving.

"It's fine. There's a hot hockey player serving it for charity. Apparently, he came over from the Lake Spark Spinners," Brooke casually mentions, and Grayson gives his wife an odd look.

"Mom. You cougar, you." Rosie is joking around.

"That's your mom. Breaking hearts in her prime." He kisses Brooke's cheek.

It's all a little too cutesy for me, but it is the festive season.

"How's the campaign going?" Grayson asks.

Now I have to chuckle. "Easy. Not much to challenge, as Pete Smythe only hands out cookies. It's my parents who take this way more seriously than me. I let them do it because they're retired and need some entertainment."

Rosie touches my chest affectionately. "Carter is going to

ensure we have a new bench right over there." She points down the street.

"Someone knows what to do with power," her father jokes.

Her mom touches Rosie's stomach. "We're getting closer. Have you thought more about your birth plan?"

"I've just been doing my yoga to ensure I stay flexible, and my breathing is strong. I will skip all of those baby classes. I want natural, with candles and music. Maybe in a bathtub. I'll be sure to drink a lot of raspberry tea the weeks before. I should probably make my oil blend to put on my pulse points." Rosie lists everything as if it's a shopping list for the store.

Grayson and I share a look because we have no clue what Rosie just rattled off, but it's definitely her and all of her quirks.

I hug her from the side. "I'll just show up."

"Good plan," Grayson concurs.

"I'm excited for the baby shower, even if due to a certain mother, we've had to move the party to your friend's." Brooke shoots me her disapproval.

I hold my hands up in surrender. "What? She might be my mom, but it doesn't mean I can control her."

"Fine. But please warn your mother dearest that I'm handling the desserts. She doesn't seem to grasp that."

Rosie and I just look at one another and try not to laugh.

"Enough of that. How are you two doing?" Grayson asks.

Rosie plays with her mitten. "You know…" Her voice squeaks. "It goes. Oh my goodness, is there fresh popcorn over there? And Gracie is here. We need to go say hi." She quickly detours the conversation before she rushes off, dragging her mother with her.

That's an unfair move because now I'm stuck with Grayson alone. I smile warily at him.

"Oh, look at that. You and me." He seems pleased with this.

"So it seems." I'm sensing a man-to-man conversation coming my way.

He crosses his arms. "Carter, soon you're going to be a father. Rosie is my firstborn. She came into my life when I wasn't expecting it, a bright light bringing Brooke and me even closer after years apart. I've been in your shoes. The difference is that you two were married, and Rosie is a free spirit who needs re-assurance and follows her own path until she finds the end. You realize that, right?" His tone is fragile because he's talking about his daughter.

"Grayson, that's why I'm being patient. Throwing her over my shoulder and insisting we get married again because we're going to be parents isn't the way to do it. I'm not going to force her hand in marriage."

"You're right. You should only marry if it's something right. Still…" He lifts a shoulder. "I would be lying if I said that I don't want to see you both as husband and wife again."

I bite inside my cheek, trying to prevent the slip of my lips to display how this is a serious moment, but so help me, I want to grin. "Is this when you tell me that I have your approval?"

"Well, you sure as hell didn't ask me last time. But yeah, it's something like that."

"Thanks, but I already married her once without your approval, so I'm good."

He grimaces at me, maybe half appreciative of that comment.

With Brooke and Rosie appearing again, Grayson and I give one another a nod in understanding.

"What were you two talking about?" Rosie is curious, and her eyes skate between her father and me with a bag of popcorn in her hand.

"Oh, nothing," he lies. "Just wondering if he needed help with the baby's room. Painting or something like that. Your uncles are making a crib for you. I was wondering what color, but Carter wouldn't budge on the boy-girl issue."

Rosie smiles proudly to all of us. "He's keeping to his word and not giving a peep of a clue."

That I am.

I wrap my arm around Rosie's shoulders and side-hug her. "I'll let you guys have a bit of time together. My dad is somewhere around here." I flash a smile at Brooke. "My mom went to see a friend up in Chicago for the weekend to shop."

The battle of the moms war runs strong, even though they do get along… I think.

"Oh goody," she replies dryly.

Rosie just rolls her eyes before I walk back into the crowd that are all gathered around the Christmas tree that just appeared today.

My friends are here somewhere, but it will only be a quick hello. People stop me for small talk which makes my search for my dad become a trudge through the crowd. Finally, fifteen minutes later, my father waves to me up ahead, trying to grab my attention, and I indicate with my hand that I see him. When I arrive next to him, I hear the tail end of a conversation that he's having with one of his old business associates, with my dad enthusiastic as he speaks.

"Obviously, the next step is Congress. Carter has the congressional district, as he was sheriff over in Lake Spark for a while. Everybody knows him. I'm not sure why he doesn't just skip being mayor."

John Doyle smiles at me and shakes my hand. He attends

my parents' holiday party every year. "I've got to agree with your father. You're well known around the area. I don't know anyone who has a negative thing to say about you. Even Pete struggles to come up with an attack. He's only mentioned that you and your ex-wife don't have your relationship in order. But nobody around here cares about that stuff."

My dad points his finger up. "In Congress they might."

John scoffs it off. "And? We'll just make sure that Carter has a strong campaign team and donors."

I'm not sure they even realize that I'm still here or that they're plotting my future together.

"Would you like me to add to this conversation or are you two all good?"

My father slaps a hand on my shoulder. "Sorry, Son, we're getting carried away."

"Ya think?" I comment flatly.

"Carter, this time next year you will have your new title as mayor, and the deputy sheriff will get his promotion which will make him happy. All things fall into place," John adds.

I rub my face and realize that my gloves are still stuffed in my coat pockets, and it connects that I haven't thought about my fingers freezing because every male here has decided to voice their opinions to me.

"Congress. I'll consider it when I'm in office, okay? It's still a few years away."

"Unless you resign as mayor to run for Congress or even Senate." My father continues to voice his strategy, and I'm getting a headache.

Pete Smythe, my opponent, steps into our circle, interrupting our conversation. "That would mean he would need to travel to Springfield even more, and D.C., too. Not exactly ideal for a young family. Now, is it?"

The guy has the farmers' vote, though sadly for him,

that's not enough backing. Doesn't matter, I'll still ensure they have the town's support.

"Thank you for your concern." I smile tightly.

"I'm sure my daughter-in-law is up to the challenge of being a politician's wife." My father has no qualms to show his confidence, and I don't have the energy to remind him that Rosie is still my ex-wife.

John squeezes my arm. "Your father is right." His tone sings.

I throw my hands in the air. "Can we focus on the festive season? There are gingerbread cookies somewhere or a candy cane, perhaps. Maybe Santa would like to listen about my wish list of getting out of this conversation."

The men chuckle around me.

"Always a joker, this one." My father grins to himself.

A deep breath doesn't seem to give them a clue that the discussion is closed, but luckily, Rosie slowly walking into our circle is the cure.

"Evening, gentlemen." Her smile thins.

They all greet her, but before anybody can drag her into this, I speak. "You must be tired. We should go home. It's been a long day, and you need your rest." I touch her arm, eager for my escape opportunity. "Bye, everyone. I'll call you this weekend, Dad." I string the sentence together and don't even wait for a response.

Rosie watches me strangely when we are far enough away, and a long audible exhale bursts out of me.

"Wow. I seemed to walk in at the wrong time."

I shake my head and drag my hand across my face. "No. Perfect timing. Where are your parents?"

"They went home. We'll see them soon. Can we go back to the house? I am a little tired."

"Yeah, sure, are you okay?" I touch her shoulder,

concerned, and study her. She seems different, but I can't pinpoint it. Her scarf is in place, and her cheeks have the same shade of pink she had before due to the cold. Her beanie over her long hair is still perfectly set.

"Totally. It's just cold." She's lying, I can tell.

But I let her lead the way.

———

EVEN THOUGH IT'S a five-minute drive home, Rosie's subdued mood doesn't go unnoticed. Something is off, and when we're inside and she tosses her hat into the basket next to the coats that we just hung, then I'm positive she's in a mood.

She even ignores me when she begins to march to the stairs, until I stop her by grabbing her arm.

"Talk to me."

She heaves a sigh. "Is it true? That you want to run for Congress, Senate, God knows what else? I thought it's just mayor."

"It is."

"But would you want to one day be more?"

I shrug and wonder where the hell we're going with this conversation. "I can't say."

"Well, your father seems to think so, and he also seems to think that I'll be a good politician's wife. I won't. I'm… a little eccentric." She flutters her eyes and lines form on her face.

A smirk begins to play on my lips. "Is that what has you bothered?" I gently walk her off the step and wind her into my arms. "I assure you that we shouldn't listen to my father's fantasies. I mean, maybe one day he's right, but for now, I'm okay right where I am."

She pouts and peers down at her belly that's growing by the day, it seems. "Still, I'm just not ready to sign up to be *that* kind of politician's wife. Mayor duties where you pet the state-winning cow is more me, you know."

Nibbling my bottom lip, I love that I'm about to point out the obvious. "You know you keep saying wife."

Her eyes pop out, and her gaze rockets up to me. "I didn't."

"You did."

"You're mistaken." She attempts to hold a weak self-assured smile.

"Hmm." My head bobs. "I think you did."

She grows flustered, and her jaw slides side to side as her hands pump fists. "If I did, it's your fault."

I step back, astonished and amused. "My fault? How?"

"You're the one who has rings upstairs. It just confused my brain for a second."

"Really? Is this the part where I'm supposed to forget your little slip-up?"

She growls and pushes me out of the way, beelining it to the living room where she paces back and forth in front of the fireplace. "Carter, I have pregnancy brain. I forget things. It's a side effect, you know."

I flop onto the sofa to enjoy the view of her little meltdown. "You said it more than once." Now I'm just egging her on.

She grabs a cushion then throws it at me, and I dodge it. "Maybe. Fine…" she drawls, giving up. "I said wife. It's a figure of speech. Most definitely not because I once had that title or one day I'll have it again." Her hand flies to mouth, too late to catch her sentence.

Refraining from allowing her to mull over her confession

for too long, I hold out my arms, inviting her to join me on the sofa. To my surprise, she joins me, defeated.

I would have her lie on top of me, but that baby bump is a little obstacle. Instead, I rub her back when she sits next to me. My cheeks rise from the smirk of satisfaction that I'm attempting to tamp down.

"It's okay. Obviously, it's on your mind, even if you don't want to admit it. I'm not going to go grab the rings. We don't need to rush," I promise with a struggle.

She side-eyes me before returning to staring down at her belly. "Fine. I confess that it floats into my mind. It's crazy because we should be going slow, but that speed doesn't feel right."

I kiss the top of her head that has a faint hint of the smell of burning wood from the bonfire in town. "Want to know a secret?" I whisper against her forehead.

"Surprise me."

"I think about it almost every hour."

Her head reangles as she studies me. "Being remarried isn't the end all. We've circled back to one another and the baby is a bonus. But being remarried doesn't need to be the sign that we're okay again."

I run my thumb down her arm. "You just let it slip a minute ago what your subconscious is thinking, though," I highlight.

She can't challenge me and nibbles her bottom lip, and her eyes appear to gleam with joy. "What do we do now?" She wants me to give her the answer.

For a woman who is independent and spirited, when she wants me to provide answers and guide our way, it feels it's because I have years on her to make me smarter.

It's not true. I'm just in love with this woman and will do anything to make her happy and ensure she is in my arms. I made one misstep when I signed those papers, and fuck, I won't make another mistake.

Her entire body melts into me, and she sniffles, a tear emerging from her eye. "I was being so silly thinking that you only wanted to be with me because of your political career."

"Rosie. You're under this roof and with me not because of career or our baby. It's because I love you and never stopped."

Her crying is bearable only because she's grasping what she needs to hear and has been obvious all along but never said out loud.

She swipes away a tear with the back of her hand, and my thumb stops a drop on her other cheek.

"I never stopped loving you either. Maybe that's why I wonder if we should have space. I don't want to hurt you again."

I shift on the couch to catch her sight and trap her hands between my own. "If you dare do that then I'll lose my mind, and I won't let you pack a single suitcase. I'll even throw them out."

She sniffles another tear. "I'm sure you would."

"We don't need to do anything. You've said you love me and mentioned wife at some point." She pinches my arm because I'm teasing her. "Our day is complete, and we can go to bed finally at peace that we're not hiding anything from one another."

Her chuckle mixed with snot makes her more lovable. "You're still kind of keeping a major secret that involves pink or blue."

I bring her hands up and kiss them. "That shall not be shared."

"You're unbreakable, aren't you?"

"Only you can break me, but you can also put me back together."

Her eyes glisten with more tears. "I'm scared. I don't want to break us again."

Dropping our hands, I kiss her lips with urgency and firmness to make it clear that she's wrong. "No need to be. I'm here."

"I've missed you, and I kind of missed mentioning that sometime in the last few months." Her face goes cartoonish with her swollen eyes.

"I kind of got the memo when we slept together the first time and created a baby."

She bubbles a laugh and plays along. "Oh good, I thought I wasn't clear enough."

Another kiss and then one more. Standing, I offer her my hand and then tug her up. I lead us straight up the stairs in silence and directly to our room.

With our eyes speaking their own language, I slowly undress her, and she does the same to me.

We lie on the bed. Rosie gets comfortable on her side with a pillow propped under her head and another in front of her that she throws her leg over. She's perfectly shaped to the bed to be comfortable and easy for me to take her from behind.

Lying behind her, she meets my gaze again because her head can twist slightly, and she captures my lips for a kiss.

My hand follows the curve of her side and over the slope of her belly. The moment I touch her clit, my cock is harder than rock.

One finger enters her, and I take note of how warm she is and the way her body has been changing. Her tits have been driving me crazy as they get bigger.

But right now, I touch her pussy for a little bit while our eyes gravitate to one another and our mouths feather.

"I love you," I mutter and barely touch her chin.

Sliding into her with my cock, she's snug, and her walls clench around my length as I thrust gently, just halfway, and then returning deep within her. Agonizing for us both, but we're not going fast tonight.

"I love you," she whispers and chases my lips.

Another pump and this time deeper. I'm cautious that she's extra sensitive and maybe in an uncomfortable way due to our baby growing, and that's why I'm delicate with Rosie. I show restraint when all I want to do is fill her to the hilt with one blunt thrust.

Instead, I take my time and appreciate her body. Cupping her breast, nuzzling into the curve of her neck, scraping her shoulder with my teeth until she interlaces our fingers and rests them on her belly.

Time stops, and we stay this way until we both shudder, and even then, I keep her tightly close and remain inside of her.

She hums a sound before she dozes off, and I kiss her shoulder and follow her shortly after.

This is where we're supposed to be.

16
ROSIE

My leg is high in the air as I move through my one-legged downward dog. I can't help but notice a pair of heavy eyes glued to me in my side view, of a man in uniform.

I huff out a sound of annoyance and give up on my pose. Standing tall, I set my hands on my hips and give Carter a pointed stare. "What?"

"I don't think you should be doing all of this."

Kicking the yoga mat on the living room floor, I'm exasperated and a little cranky. "We've gone over this. I'm fine. It's good to keep my body limber, too. Besides, the baby loves it. Always gives a little kick when I'm relaxing after my sequences."

Carter moseys on past me and leans down to roll up the mat. "I'm sure. But you are basically doing splits half the time and balancing on one foot."

"*Grrr*," I growl. "Will you stop being an overprotective freak? Otherwise, I might throw a few of your trolls into the snow outside." Even if he is being so ridiculously endearing.

He chuckles at me as he sets my mat in the corner and

checks that I'm not burning down the house with the candles that I've lit. "Except that you've been using them as Elf on the Shelf. I know you've been moving the Krampus troll."

"No. I'm moving that because it's creepy. The evil version of Santa needs to not be in this house."

Carter walks to me and holds me from behind. My head falls in place against his shoulder.

We managed to keep everyone at bay at Christmas. Small family dinner one day and another the other day to cover our bases. Every single person's gift to us was a tiny stocking for the fireplace. Nobody seemed to check with one another, so now we have six different stockings to choose from.

"I'll start packing up the decorations when I'm back from work." His voice spreads across my skin just below my earlobe.

"We still have New Year's Eve. It can wait until tomorrow." I rub his forearms resting on my stomach.

"If you're not up when I'm back, it's okay. You've been tired."

I laugh. "I'll be up for midnight or just wake me up. Starting a fresh new year with you is perfect."

"You also said that about every single new moon, full moon, blue moon, and probably some other moon that I've never heard of," he notes.

Wiggling in his arms, I respond to his teasing. "True. But a new year is a new year. A long cycle. Last year was full of surprises. Tomorrow, we wake knowing our baby is no longer a surprise, where I live is no longer a surprise, and we'll be focusing on nesting and enjoying the newborn phase. See? All planned, and we should celebrate that."

He kisses my cheek before letting me go. "I'm following along with your logic because you're carrying our child. I'll be back."

I wave my fingers in the air as acknowledgment that I heard him while he disappears upstairs. Meandering to the kitchen, I'm on the search for pink wafer cookies and some carrots because it's the perfect combo in my book.

Finding the dry cookie in the jar, I snort a laugh to myself because out the window I see pawprints in the thin layer of snow in the back. There is no Jet in sight, but clearly, he escaped and was here. One crunchy bite and I ease into a lazy afternoon. I hear Carter zip down the stairs, and the door shuts right after.

This happens a lot lately since I've been teaching less. Minutes where I stop and immerse myself in my surroundings. It's no longer Carter's house; it feels like a home. The days are routine, and I don't mind.

It causes my mouth to etch a smile.

When I was married to Carter, every day was a little spontaneous. There was less structure because I wanted to go with the flow. Now? Some things fall into blocks during the day, and I'm okay with that. It's actually pretty damn enjoyable.

Puzzle pieces eventually fall into place. Even if there are hundreds. With Carter, we only had a few, but it took a while to lay them out.

We're running out of the final pieces to place.

And that's a good sign.

VAGUELY, the heaviness of someone close to me causes me to stir groggily in bed. I'm struggling in an attempt to wake, and instead, sigh blissfully and keep my head comfy against the fluffy pillow for my sleepy slumber.

There is a briskness to the cool air inside the bedroom,

but underneath the blankets, it's toasty and warm. My uncovered shoulders feel warmth now cascading down my skin.

I hum a sound and feel the gruffness of Carter's stubble. Even with the tip of his nose sensually snuggling against my skin, I refuse to wake fully.

There is no need.

Everything feels right.

His arms wrap around me as he spoons me from behind, and our hands find the spot on my stomach that we always touch when sleep takes over us.

"Happy New Year," he whispers.

Mumbling something back, I return to my dream.

———

My eyes squint open to light from outside. Rubbing my eyes, I yawn and notice that it's morning with clouds outside, as half of the blinds are raised. I slept heavenly, which explains why the clock says 9:30 in the morning and I'm only just waking up.

The sound of someone in the other room instantly makes me happy because it's Carter. Using my arms, I begin to sit up on my side. One more yawn, and I realize that I completely missed the stroke of midnight.

It's disappointing, but a good night's sleep isn't half bad either.

Stretching my arms up in the air, I set my feet on the floor and kick on one unicorn slipper then the next. I quickly go to the bathroom and grab a sweater and opt for staying in my pajamas. Before the baby, I loved to chill in leggings and t-shirts, and with a baby, my style hasn't changed because it's now a necessity.

The moment that I pause at the door of the small bedroom

that will become the baby's nursery, my entire heart melts all over again.

Carter throws me a glance mid brush stroke, painting the wall. "Morning. Welcome to a new year."

I laugh. "I missed it, didn't I?"

"Yeah, I wanted you to sleep, though." He sets the brush by the side of the canister on plastic covering the floor before he comes to give me a kiss.

Jabbing a finger into his chest, I can't break this grin that beams on my face. "You picked the paint color without me!" It's a light beige which makes sense and will go well with creams, but still. "Love the communication on this one," I say, sarcastic.

"Relax." He curls his fingers around my pointer finger and brings the pad of my finger to his lips for a kiss. "I know you don't care, now get the hell out of here. The paint fumes aren't good for you. I thought I would paint the accent wall that we talked about. I've been awake since six."

I crane my neck and appraise the wall behind him. "It does look great."

"See? Now go away. Have breakfast, and I'll be down in a bit."

"Fine. But only because I'm hungry."

He smirks with satisfaction and shoos me away.

It isn't until an hour later that he joins me downstairs, freshly showered and in sweats. I'm busy on the floor untangling tree lights to put them back in the box. We opted for a tiny fake tree. I'm nearly done after five minutes. Carter joins me on the floor to help.

"You're not upset about missing New Year's?"

I roll a shoulder back. "Nah. In the end, the biggest day this year will be when he or she decides to come into the world… Plus, it's a new moon next week. We're fine."

"Alright. If you say so." We succeed with the string of lights, and he places it in the storage box. "I finished the wall, and next week, I'll put the car seats in the car."

Instantly, I gush contentment. "Can't believe that in six to eight weeks this girl or boy will show up."

"Unless you go over. My mom went over with Oliver and me."

"But my mom had me early. So, who knows."

He lies on his side and props his elbow up. His brown eyes glint with a little sparkle. "In a few weeks, I'll be named mayor too."

I raise a brow at him. "Someone is a little cocky."

Carter has a cunning grin that turns me on. "I think we know where it's going to go. I bought everyone at Foxy Rox coffees last time I was there."

"Bribery, huh?"

It earns me a wink. I notice the way he's watching his fingers circle on the rug in front of him, keeping himself occupied. His throat bobs in a way that seems he's gearing himself up. "Rosie." His voice is nuanced, and his eyes flick up to meet mine. "We still haven't really talked about what you said the other day."

I could throw out a funny retort right now, but I'm aware of the significance of his question.

"You mean the wife part?" My voice is very delicate.

"Yeah. That."

Licking my lips, I debate what to say. "Is there something to talk about?"

His finger begins to draw a circle on my wrist. "I'm just wondering where your head is at. The past month has been busy, but we only seem to get better." He's desperately searching for me to say what he hopes I will.

"That's true. We haven't really mentioned it again." Probably because I've been so wrapped in how great things *are* going.

He trails his long finger from my wrist down to my empty ring finger where he stops. "Just know that before I become mayor or we have a baby, I'm saving the rings for none of those reasons to ask you to be my wife again. The rings are waiting for you because you're supposed to have them again."

My heart jumps from the yearning in his voice, with the full sincerity of what his heart wants.

Still, my eyes turn into saucers. "Is this a proposal?"

He smirks to himself. "It can be if you want it to be. It's more ensuring you have clarity on what I'm envisioning. You don't need to ask questions because I'm laying it all on the table, yours for the taking."

It is tempting to fly into his arms and say yes.

But that tiny part of me still wants to be certain that we won't hurt one another all because we got lost in a surprise fate has thrown at us.

Still, I bring my hand to his cheek and rub my finger by the corner of his mouth. "Keep holding on to the rings."

That's a promise I can make, and it's true.

Today, I'll keep an answer to myself. But I don't believe much more time is needed.

My answer is enough for him today, and he scoots a little closer to me, weaves his fingers through my hair, and dips his chin down to angle his mouth over mine for a kiss.

Sometimes kisses are the only answer we need that everything will be alright.

17
CARTER

I struggle to drag my eyes away from Rosie who is standing across the room at the River Bell, next to the window showing the freezing evening sky. It's that smile that slays or the way her blue dress exemplifies her fuller breasts that has me entranced.

I shouldn't be, as the room chatters with people drinking wine. The River Bell, the restaurant on the old paddle steamer at the dock, is sophisticated enough. Also, it's the place where one celebrates becoming mayor.

I'm wearing a suit and nursing the scotch in my hand. I tear my eyes away because Oliver is attempting to engage me in conversation.

"This will be a fucking travesty if you don't win. Mom and Dad over there will be in meltdown mode and trying to find a loophole to recall the election."

We both glance to the corner of the room, where our parents are chatting with former business associates, all with wide grins on their faces. The private room with appetizers and drinks floating around is mostly enjoyed by their guests and a few who own small businesses or have a farm out of town.

Smirking to myself, I have to agree. "What can I say? I'm not exactly lacking confidence on this."

My brother bubbles a chuckle. "Someone is a little too cocky."

"I'm just being realistic. Last I heard, I already had most of the votes. Hell, even Pete Smythe already shook my hand earlier out on Main Street because he knew I will most likely win."

He bobs his head side to side. "It's a solid point." His eyes travel between Rosie and me because my sight has drifted again. "Uh… is it official yet that you two are back together and regretting your divorce?"

Oliver has an impeccable capability of throwing cold water on me to break me away from the contentment of the current day. I side-eye him, not at all impressed. "Here isn't the time to talk about this. I have the owner of Foxy Rox to talk to and discuss small business incentives." Yet, I don't move. I ponder. "We're living together, having a baby, no longer in separate rooms, communicating and open, isn't that enough?" It's not, not really. She needs to have my name again, and my clock runs fast. But maybe the image of what we currently are is enough for other's opinions, even though I don't care. I just want them to hush their views.

"All great signs. I mean, the moment she re-entered your life you were no longer the man who mopes around grumpy. It's just, you're my brother, so I know that you are pining for something more. It's not rocket science."

I chuff a sound. "Tell that to Rosie," I admit. "For someone who normally throws caution to the wind, she's now a bit more practical when it comes to marriage, more reserved, yet still burning cinnamon sticks around the house."

"We all grow."

I tut my tongue then take another sip of my drink, driving my sight to Rosie who's laughing with Esme and Hailey as she looks down at her belly that she rubs. For a second, our eyes catch, and her smile might even brighten a little.

"I'm trying to respect her timeline, but I'm about to lose my damn mind."

Olivers squeezes my shoulder. "That's because you never actually let her go. Hang in there. Besides, you have a town to run now. And Mom to deal with. Alert. Alert. Woman who bore us at 12 o'clock."

"Boys," our mother sings in her chipper tone as she walks to us with her fitted black dress and necklace with a diamond pendant. "I hope you two are behaving. We have just received a call that my son is a man in government now." My mom eagerly gives me a side-hug.

"I've always worked for the government. I'm a police officer," I deadpan.

Logic washes over her face, and she shutters her eyes. "Of course, silly me."

"Are the votes in?" Oliver asks.

"They are." She grins.

Truthfully, this news gives me a sense of pride that races through me, and I feel the corner of my mouth snag.

She directs her attention to my brother. "You need to go grab the new mayor's wife for us. Be my favorite youngest son and do that for me?"

Oliver smirks slyly to himself. "Not quite his wife, but sure. I'll stir the pot for ya." He strolls aways, and I force a smile to my overexcited mother.

"Your father is ensuring champagne is passed around for a little toast, photos and handshakes, all of those kinds of things. I'm so proud of you. Mayor and soon-to-be father. I noticed Rose seems thrilled to be here. Once the baby is here then I'm sure she will fall right into the role of holding your arm while you give a speech at the town's July Fourth picnic. Speaking of which, it's a blue blanket that I need to get, right?" she causally throws in.

I smirk. "Nice try, but I'm not saying."

My mother wiggles her finger at me and grins. "You don't want to tell your dear old mom? I won't tell a soul."

"You would be the last person I trust."

She lets me off without further investigation because our attention turns to Rosie who joins us. "Congratulations." Her ear-to-ear smile mirrors my own before she gives me a hug.

"Thanks." I appreciate how she naturally settles next to me, in the perfect spot for my hand to find home on her lower back. Her radiant smile between us all is a bonus, too.

"Ready?" Rosie asks me, while my mother waves to my father. The way Rosie peers up to me from my side, forcing me to glance down, is perfect.

"Nothing to be nervous about. I'm sorry if they plant you next to me for the next hour for photos."

She stifles a laugh. "Mayor posing next to his baby mama," she mutters.

I squeeze her close to me. "Don't make me want to reprimand you right now," I taunt her under my breath, and my long fingers cascade a little lower to borderline inappropriate on her lower back.

My father is thrilled when a tray of champagne arrives to add to the celebration. He is quick to shove a glass into my hand, while my mother offers Rosie a glass of orange juice.

Maybe I do have a few tiny butterflies inside of me. This is a career shift, after all. A milestone in someone's life. Okay, maybe there is a little adrenaline, too. Fine, it's excitement.

With one ding from my father's glass using a cocktail fork, the room grows quiet. "If I can have your attention, I think we can celebrate what we all came here for," he says, addressing the room. "It's a great day for Everhope. I received a call to confirm, please join me in a toast for our new mayor, Carter Oaks." He glances over his shoulder at me and lifts his glass. "I couldn't be prouder of my son."

The moment everyone claps, Rosie joins in, and I kiss her cheek while I bask in the fact that everyone is staring at me.

"Congratulations, Son. How about a few words." It's not a request from my father, it's a cue.

Dropping my hand from Rosie's back, I wait while the claps die down. Holding up my glass, I begin a speech that I didn't practice except for a sentence or two. "Thank you everyone, for your vote and for being here with me to celebrate. To my parents, brother, friends, and most of all, Rosie, my…" My smile stalls, and I'm not sure what to say. Maybe people notice the moment of awkwardness in the air, and Rosie softly gawks her eyes at me. "Who I'm having a baby with." It's true. "I look forward to helping Everhope and ensure we stay the great little town we are. It's an honor to serve you just as I have as sheriff, which is still a member of government." I throw my gaze at my mother whose smile strains. "Cheers, everyone."

The room clinks glasses with one another, and the buzz of conversations returns after people take sips of their drinks.

Rosie leans into me and touches our flutes. "Nice save there," she teases me quietly.

"Well, we could rectify that title any moment," I remind her.

She shakes her head playfully. Her demeanor changes to serious. "Congratulations, Carter, on becoming mayor."

I side-hug her and lean down to kiss the top of her head. "Thanks."

Before I can say more, a photographer appears before us, and she's already adjusting her camera strap. My mother is encouraging Rosie to squeeze tighter into me.

"There we go. Perfect," my mother is directing. "A smidgen closer perhaps."

Rosie just finds it all hilarious. "Obvious much?" she whispers to me.

We give her three poses to fulfill the quota, and then she is dragging my brother and Hailey into the picture, along with my dad, and it's a full-on family photo.

After a few photos, everyone is freed from my mother's demands.

"Not you, Carter. We need some solo photos and, of course, with some others here." My mother stops me from taking any movements.

But Rosie does, and she steps back. "She's right. You have mayor responsibilities to fulfill now. Besides, I'm going to head home, and you can stay here. Hailey said she'll take me. I'm tired." She's still smiling at me, and her words speak truth; she's not trying to run.

I touch her shoulders, and my eyes drop to her lips then draw a line back to her eyes. "Of course. I'm not sure how long I'll be, but don't wait up. You're carrying important cargo." I wink at her.

She closes our space. "Yeah, yeah, yeah." She rises up on her toes to steal a kiss from me.

The kiss lasts longer than it should for public settings, but I don't care.

Rosie pulls away, and her thumb draws a quick circle on my cheek. "Congratulations again, Mayor. We're proud of you."

We both drop our eyes to the view of the big bump between us.

"Go on. Get some rest," I insist.

Rosie strokes my arm once, and our fingers graze before we part.

And I still can't help but notice her bare finger.

———

STANDING the doorway of my bedroom, I heave a sigh from the evening. It only took what felt like a thousand handshakes and chitchat conversations before I could escape. Now, I'm looking at Rosie sitting up in bed on top of the duvet, scrolling on her tablet to look at her baby inspiration mood board. She glances up and smiles to herself.

"You look like a man who is eager to get into bed, and I'm not entirely sure it's for any activity other than sleep," she comments then sets her tablet on the side table.

Walking into the room, I begin to undress. "That sounds like a challenge."

A smirk plays on her lips. "Maybe."

I huff a laugh. "Are we still in the insatiable part of the pregnancy?"

She begins to shift in bed and appears sultry and eager. "No. We're in the I want to celebrate with you part of the pregnancy."

My brows rise. "Oh yeah?" I step out of my pants and take no notice where they land after I toss them to the side.

She's crawling on all fours toward the edge of the bed. "Yeah." Her tone is floaty. "Now get on your back."

Fuck it. I take off every scrap of clothing that I have and do as she says, my cock hard and straight up at her disposal.

Without missing a beat, I lie down, and she swings one

leg over my hips, and in my own frenzy of undressing, she took off her own clothes.

We've had to ditch any positions where she is on her back, which, truthfully, has kind of been a win for me. Because here I am with Rosie on top of me, with her breasts full and the slope of her belly defined. A tantalizing goddess, as always.

She swivels her pussy over my lap, and a need to slam her down on top of my cock claws inside of me.

"You were kind of hot back there in your mayor glory. I might miss the handcuffs, but this is the next best thing."

I sit up to kiss her. "We can keep the handcuffs," I rasp.

My lips dust down her neck to the valley between her breasts, before I suck one nipple then move on to the other. I don't linger for long because Rosie doesn't give me a chance. Instead, she pushes my chest back until I'm lying underneath her.

"Want a confession?" she whispers.

"Absolutely."

She lifts her hips just enough then lowers her pussy onto my tip. "I've been wanting to do this all night."

She slides down my cock, and we both croon from the instant feel of her pussy encasing me. She clenches, and I'm close due to the rush of blood to my cock. She clamps harder and makes me a man unhinged. My eyes meet hers, and I attempt to disarm any idea in her head that she will get to do this alone.

My fingers run along her hipbones to her ass as she continues to rock her hips.

"You make me lose my mind," I whisper.

The way she combs her fingers and pulls up her hair, only to let it all fall behind her shoulders is so fucking gorgeous.

Her nails claw into my chest as she bounces, her moans

mingling with mine. I'm desperate to take control so I can nip at those peaked nipples. But she has me chained to the bed with her eyes, well aware that my dick is throbbing, and she is the only one to save me.

It's a few minutes of heaven before my vision begins to litter with colored dots, and my body bursts when I come inside of her, our breaths now ragged and pulses high.

Rosie has a talent for making me fall for her all over again and then again.

Her lips seal against mine when I sit up, and I haven't left her body. "That was…" I take control of my breath.

"Hmm." She's turning groggy as she does after sex. The perfect way to relax. So much so that our bodies shake off all worries.

Orgasms cause us not to think, as we are in a trance.

But eventually we snap out of it.

It's a few minutes later, when I'm in bed sitting up and waiting for Rosie to return from the bathroom. That haunting feeling returns to me. The urge to ask yet another time.

I debate if I should grab her ring, and it doesn't take long. I dart out of bed and grab the piece of jewelry that is a ghost from the past.

Setting it right where I want it to be, I wait patiently in bed, and when Rosie returns in her pajamas, I act natural.

"I bet you I don't get to sleep. This baby will wake me at 2am for kicks and a party." She yawns, and when she turns the edge of the duvet on her side over, she instantly freezes before she scoffs. "Really?" She doesn't sound so thrilled.

We both stare at the ring that I left on her pillow.

"Yes, really. I'm breaking a promise, and I can't help it, I'm going to keep bringing it up."

She doesn't enter the bed, instead her eyes swimming between the ring and me. "Carter, I said be patient."

I lean across the mattress to grab her arm, but she dodges my efforts. "And I'm impatient. We're opposites. Now, tell me what's really bothering you?"

She avoids my eyes lasering in on her, her entire body language saying that she's struggling internally with something.

Then it happens.

Something inside of her snaps. She picks up the ring and sets it on the table at the side of the bed with the sound bellowing through the room. "Because I regret what I did. I'm the one who ruined us. I'm scared I will do it again." It shoots out of her mouth until she realizes it all rolled off her tongue, and the air grows stiff.

Her eyes droop to the floor with remorse, and I scoot closer to her as she stands next to the bed. My hand captures the side of her soft face, slightly cold from the brisk winter evening and the heating on low. "We just grew apart. It might have felt as though we needed closure at some point, but we never did because we were supposed to circle back to one another. I made mistakes too."

"Only because I felt the need to explore and was careless with your feelings."

I tug her wrist my way. "Hey, look at me." Her eyes slowly sweep up to meet mine. "You also left a trail so I could find you again."

Rosie rolls her lips in, soaking in my words, but I still see the struggle for her to accept what she hears. "Carter..." Her voice cracks, and she gathers my hand to hold between both of hers. "Your belief in us is the most beautiful and promising thing. It's also my downfall because I never want to hurt you. I said I'm almost there about re-marriage. That's still true."

I sigh. "Just not yet."

She kisses my palm gently and doesn't let my hand go. "I

love you so much that I want to ensure that you have it all without any little cracks. Just give me a little time, okay?"

My mouth stretches a weak line in acknowledgment.

Rosie begins to wobble on her knees on the mattress as I scoot back. We both find our spots under the covers with a swirl of awkwardness in the air.

It's a few seconds until she does what she's good at, breaking tension with a smile.

She nudges my arm as we sit side by side. "Point for proposal creativity, though." She lifts a brow at me with a wry smile.

"Points for celebrating my career win," I counter because it was good sex, and my disappointment erases off my face.

She giggles and kisses my cheek. "You'll still let me steal a pillow?"

I shake my head and my mouth stretches. "It's for the baby, so I'm not going to say no." Rosie requires a lot of pillows these days to get comfortable on her side.

"Thank you. I promise not to steal any blankets."

"How considerate of you." We both shuffle into our spots to get comfortable for the night.

Once she's snuggling in, I take a few extra beats to stroke her cheek once, and she nips my thumb.

"We'll be okay," she whispers.

Sighing, I know she's right. Doesn't mean I'm any less in the chokehold that this woman has always had on me or the fact that I yearn for her as my wife again.

For now, I hold her as we settle into another night of sleep.

Together.

18
ROSIE

A photo can speak truths.

That's what Esme just told me.

Maybe that's why an overwhelming feeling has been chasing me for days.

"Okay, let's move from the bed to the window. It will be a perfect shot," she directs me with her camera in one hand.

We're in her studio, also known as the spare bedroom in her old house. Boudoir and engagement shoots are her talent. When she suggested that I have a little shoot half naked while pregnant, it was an instant yes from me.

"By the window is a good idea," I agree.

I have super fluffy socks on, panties, and a black bra visible under an open-button shirt that falls to my thighs and displays my belly. The chilly winter day streams light into the room despite it being cloudy.

"Stand sideways and pretend to look out the window."

Following instruction, I get into the pose and relish this scenario, as it's exactly what I wanted. The clicking of her lens should make this feel unnatural, but her talent and my confidence have made this anything but.

"Ready for your baby shower this weekend?"

I stunt a laugh. "Yes, but I've heard rumors that Hailey is worn out from calming the moms."

"She might have mentioned that she was debating slipping tranquilizers into their drinks," she jokes.

"I'm sure they will quiet down when I explain a few rituals that we are going to do. Carter's mom isn't a fan of my spiritual stuff, and my mom, bless her, always goes along for the ride."

Esme tips her eyes up quickly, and she wears a smirk before she studies her screen again. "How are you and Carter doing? You both seem to be in a good place."

It's impossible to hide it when a bright smile hits me. "We are. I'm sure he would have us remarried already if I would let us."

He's both persistent and patient. His faith in us is unwavering and causes me to believe that we are strong. But I refuse to let us down in case we're going too fast. With utmost certainty is when I will take my ring back.

It's not that we have to get married to have a loving relationship and raise a baby. It's just that it would feel as though we are missing a piece because we were once complete as husband and wife until I veered off track. I am meant to be his wife. I do believe in that. I don't think it's due to emotions related to the pregnancy that has me in that view.

"Well, everyone goes at their own pace. Keats and I took a year until we married. He's a complete family man, but I refused to try to get pregnant on the honeymoon. If he'd had it his way, then I would have already been pregnant then, but instead, I'm pre—" Her head perks when she realizes it just flowed out of her mouth.

Instantly, I have the widest grin of the day. "Pregnant?"

She can't help but smile shyly and nods.

I'm to her in a heartbeat to give her hug. "Congratulations."

She lifts her shoulders. "Thanks. I don't think I was supposed to let that slip. We're still ten weeks."

I zip my lips. "Your secret's safe with me. How are you feeling? Morning sickness?"

"No. Not at all. Not even once. Nor any other symptoms."

My jaw hangs open at how unfair that is. "Geez, I must have had morning sickness for the entire Everhope population."

She chuckles and reviews the screen on the back of her camera again. "Sorry, I shouldn't have rubbed that in. If it's any consolation, I doubt I'm going to be a unicorn like you who I think I literally saw doing the splits the other day, despite being ready to birth a child."

To be honest, that makes me proud. "Well, we'll see how I do if the baby decides to go off script during labor or I decide an epidural is more my thing. I have no illusions. No matter how I prepare, the baby will come into the world the way it needs to." I affectionately drop my eyes to my stomach.

"That's a good mindset. Still have no clue if it's a boy or girl?"

"Nah. Carter isn't budging and even plays games with me. One moment he has me thinking it's a girl and the next a boy. It's fun."

"No offence, but there is no effing way that any sane couple can do this. Points to you guys. Anyhow, how does it feel to be the girlfriend of Mr. High Powerful Mayor?"

I laugh. "Well, he isn't yet. He'll take office after the baby is born and the deputy sheriff can take on his new promotion. I'm thankful that it's Everhope. I doubt Carter will be called at two in the morning to take part in political espionage or something like that."

"I hope not," she agrees.

He's happy. I can see it every time he talks about his new position. Quite frankly, I'm excited to be on the ride with him.

A knock on the doorframe causes our eyes to fly to find Carter.

"Sorry to interrupt." His head cocks to the side as he gives me the once-over. "Actually, not really, but I heard you were here and thought I would stop by."

"I really need to lock the front door more often." Esme smirks to herself.

Carter takes a few steps into the room, and his eyes remain pinned on me. Our eyes both have a dreaminess that hasn't left for days.

"It's okay. We're pretty much finished, right?" I turn and ask Esme.

She raises her camera in her hand. "Yes, but since the father-to-be is here. Why don't I get a few photos of you two." Carter and I glance to one another with lines on our faces. "Geez, you two have your mind in the gutter. Not those kind of photos on the bed. I mean, go stand by the window, facing one another and place your hands on the belly kind of photos."

Carter doesn't need to hear another word and is already halfway to the window when I try to control the little smile that stings my lips.

Once in position, Esme continues to direct. A touch here. Eyes there. One kiss. Another.

"Rosie, these are going on the living room wall, right?" He has a devilish grin.

"Sure. Your mom, dad, brother, my parents, all want to see me half naked on the wall."

He slings his arm around me and pulls me into a squeezing hug and kisses my forehead. "Who the fuck cares. We don't exactly do conventional."

"Well, that's true."

"Totally do it," Esme comments from the sidelines.

My eyes float to Carter's, and today his eyes are the view that touches me differently. More profound. Pokes my heart then carves a feeling that will never be erased.

Esme begins to put her camera away. "I think I have plenty of photos. I'll send you a few unedited ones later today."

"Perfect," I chirp.

I'm about to step away, but Carter grabs my wrist to rein me back in. "You look beautiful, you know that, right?"

It's probably because my thoughts of him lately have cemented me to an answer that I feel is coming.

Tucking a few strands of hair behind my ear, I can't help but blush. "You need to stop saying that."

He shrugs and grins. "Well, repeating that you look like a woman who needs a ring on her finger with me as her husband probably earns me an unimpressed grimace."

Vaguely, I can hear Esme pretend to cough, clearly having heard.

As much as Carter is joking, he isn't. His wish and impatience are underneath his words.

Nervously I smile. "Well, that's my cue to get dressed and wrap this all up."

"What?" His hands come out to his sides.

Esme holds up her camera. "I mean, I do engagement photos. If it wasn't for the fact that this is my gift to you then I would say we can arrange a package deal." She is humorously throwing a little oil onto the fire, and I toss her a warning glare that causes her to chortle.

I begin to rub my temples, appearing not to enjoy this scene even though it warms my heart, and I'm struggling to lock down my smile that wants to erupt.

That's a sign. I'm not tense due to this conversation.

Carter quickly kisses my forehead. "Relax." I don't need to apparently. "Just wanted to stop by on my way to Oliver's."

"Okay, have fun."

"Just call if you need something."

I nod in acknowledgment, with a gnawing emotion inside of me.

It's only made worse when a few hours later, I'm lying on the couch with soft music, dim lighting, and a lit candle. The fleece blanket only makes my coziness even better. Carter decided to stay at Oliver's to watch the hockey on TV, as the Spinners are playing against Toronto. I think he felt guilty because we are in the last few weeks when it is just him and me before a baby enters the picture, but I assured him that I just wanted to journal then fall asleep.

The notification ding on my phone goes off, and I glance at the screen to see an incoming email from Esme. I tap my thumb on the subject line of unedited photos. The instant I see the first one, a big smile is plastered on my face.

I'm hot. I have no problem saying that.

Maybe they're right and I should hang a few photos on the wall in the living room. I'm loving my legs and arms. My hair cooperated today, too. I scroll through a few where I was sitting on my knees in the middle of the bed, a few at the window, and then I stall.

There is the photo of Carter and me together at the window. It looks natural because we don't even notice the camera, and we're smiling at one another while touching my belly. To any outsider who isn't privy to the details of our dynamics, they would only see a couple madly in love and ready to be parents.

Which is actually true.

Closing the email, I roll my lips in, and my thoughts linger for a few seconds before I tap my screen to reach the folder in my drive that I don't open often. One would think when you divorce someone that you would delete the photos, but it never crossed my mind to erase the evidence of a chapter of my life.

The screen fills with a photo of Carter and me, a selfie from our wedding day. Truely elated and in bliss. The next photo is us sitting by the river. I smile to myself at the next photo where we are lying in bed, and we were playing around with the camera one morning. Completely innocent. Fully clothed and beaming with contentment. I've started myself on a spiral as I continue to swipe. There was that time we went away to a bed-and-breakfast up in Wisconsin, and a simple photo of us drinking coffee at Jolly Joe's over in Lake Spark.

I remember the moments that are forever part of me and a reminder that I can have it all again.

That's the thing that I realize. No matter what happened or where I was or am now, Carter Oaks is like an undertow in a river. Far too strong to let you go in the opposite direction.

That never went away, nor will it ever.

19
ROSIE

My sister holds up her cake pop with icing and blue sprinkles. "So basically, we eat the balled-up cake with blue or pink sprinkles since your dearest ex-husband still won't tell anyone."

I take another bite from the blue one I have in one hand and then the pink one in my other. "You're supposed to choose the one that is your guess," I say with a full mouth.

"Sprinkles are gross." She returns to the counter to enjoy her snack plate.

I laugh then soak in the scene filled with baby shower decorations and a buffet table on one side. Hailey kept it exactly how I wanted. Not over the top.

The dining table is a mess from making candles together, but it's perfect.

My cousin, Gracie, has a faint cheeky grin on her face as she grabs a paper plate with a teddy bear on it. "So how upset is the Blisswood clan that you're not doing this at their winery?" She's busy adding vegetables to her plate.

I scoff a laugh. "About a ten, but they will get over it as

soon as someone else is knocked up or engaged, either order will do."

She takes a big bite of her carrot, causing a snapping sound. "I didn't realize how much I enjoy these parties."

"Me too," I agree.

A touch on my shoulder startles me, and the moment I turn to face Carter's mom, I force a smile. I like her, I do, but I'm well aware to brace myself for the words that are about to come out of her mouth. Gracie even gives me a humorous eye roll.

"This is a fun little get-together." I hear a but coming from my ex maybe future mother-in-law. "The candle making and need to sit barefoot on floor cushions with flower petals all around while we all share in a circle is a little… out there." She straightens her turquoise statement necklace.

My eyes fling to the table. "Your candle is nice." It's kind of ugly, but fine.

"Whatever you say. How sweet that all of the candles will be going home with you and potentially burn down my son's house." Her smile is a little on the fake side, but I will let it go. Instead of getting to host the baby shower, she compensated with a giant diaper cake, a stuffed animal the size of my body, and a stroller that is far too expensive.

"Oh, if that happens then we will just move in with you. I'm sure you won't mind having a crying baby at home again." I smile sweetly.

Her finger dabs the tip of my nose. "Always the funny one." Her smile is now honest, and we are reminded that we very much get along, even if we both have what we consider out-of-this-world ideas.

"Hopefully the baby gets that gene. Would hate for him or her to be prickly and grumpy all the time."

She chuckles under her breath. "Me too. My son can be a little uptight at times," she jokes.

I shrug. "Sometimes." Most of the time, but not with me.

Her eyes drop to my stomach, and she gushes another smile. "What a miracle. Plus, you'll have the whole street around to help. Carter will be a wonderful father, I just know it."

He will. I don't doubt that.

Nancy's eyes slide to the side, and she frowns. "Jet, get off of there," she chides. "Hailey! That mutt is eating from the counter again." She tries to shoo the dog away, and I can only grin.

Hailey rushes from across the room to grab Jet by the collar. "Sorry. He's just excited."

"I told you to keep him in the other room."

Hailey ignores her mother-in-law and leans down to scratch Jet's ears. "Not this guy. He was invited. Rosie said he can be her emotional support dog that is needed in the company of overbearing mothers." She smiles brightly.

"She's right," I add.

Hailey begins to rub Jet's cheeks. "Look at him," she coos. "Such a sweetie. I know you also brought him gourmet dog treats that you picked up in Chicago. Don't try to hide it."

Nancy rolls her eyes as her smile drives to the side. "Perhaps. Doesn't mean I want his slobber on the charcuterie board."

Jet patters away, and Hailey stands, amused. "It's fine, but I think we might be out of champagne."

"What?" Nancy is quick to answer, alarmed. "I brought twelve bottles!" She marches off in search of the alcohol.

Hailey and I just laugh at one another. She crosses her

arms and leans against the counter. "It's too easy. Especially since she means well."

I lift a shoulder. "She's just excited. It's the first grandchild. Same with my family." I softly pat my belly. "The first grandchild and grandniece or nephew for the Blisswoods."

She shrieks in excitement. "I can't wait for aunt duties."

"You'll be the fun one, and one day, he or she will go to your preschool."

She claps her hands together and jumps. "I know."

I reach out and touch her arm. "Thanks again for throwing this shower. It's perfect."

"No problem at all. I loved doing it. I hope Carter is having fun with the guys at the River Bell for drinks and dinner."

"I'm sure he is."

One of our neighbors from down the street hands Hailey a mimosa in passing, and Hailey takes a sip. "It must be super busy with the baby, mayorship, your… relationship thing." Her hand sweeps my body as her face screws. "I hope you two are having some alone time."

My head bobs. "We're trying. Tomorrow we are having dinner together. Enjoying the silence while we can."

"Enjoy sleep, too."

"Oh, I am."

My mom interrupts us. "May I steal my daughter away for a second?" She tips her head to me to indicate down the hall off the kitchen.

"Absolutely," Hailey replies.

My mom's eyes are inviting and filled with love that I imagine only a mother can have. I follow her until we are by the bottom of the stairs, without the noise of the party in the background. She hands me a bag filled with gold tissue paper.

"Something for you."

I'm curious and dip my hand inside and feel a soft animal. Pulling it out, I grin. "Jelly." My stuffed unicorn growing up.

"I figured you might need it for your baby."

Pulling the stuffed animal close to my middle, I can't shake away the sentiment of this moment. "It might not be a girl," I remind her.

"Doesn't matter. Jelly can find a place in the baby's room."

Stepping in for a big hug, I can't help but let tears form in my eyes. "Thank you."

She rubs my back as I pull away. "You know… I'm not sure if you remember, but when you were really young, you would carry the unicorn around and offer it to your father before he and I even were together. Jelly had a front-row seat to watching how our lives unfolded."

I stare at the animal for a few seconds. "I remember there was a tornado and Dad went upstairs to grab Jelly because I forgot it."

"From moment one, you had him wrapped around your finger. But we didn't come together because of you. You were just the bonus, and Jelly, too."

It's hasn't unfazed me how Carter's and my situation runs parallel to my own parents. They ended up where they were always meant to be.

"I guess Jelly gets to have a front-row seat to my current situation then."

She smirks and affectionately sweeps my hair behind my shoulders. "Nah, the unicorn is just reminding you that everything will come together… and don't worry, Jelly had a trip to the washing machine the other day. He is ready to report for duty."

I wipe a tear away. "I'm happy to hear."

"Rosie, babies happen in their own time. But everything else is in *your* own time."

Sniffling another tear, I'm going to blame this on this special day, except I can't. "I'm scared. Labor, motherhood, being a wife again."

"Labor, you have no control with. He or she will come into the world on their own terms. Every person who enters motherhood feels the same. Being a wife again with the same man, well…" Her face squinches, and it causes me to laugh and cry at the same time. "You will create your own path on that. Good news is that there is no wrong trail. There might even be a few detours."

The corner of my mouth snags as I listen to her advice that is hidden under her perspective. "I guess I have Jelly to remind me of that then."

She nods while her gaze pins to mine. "You do. Detours sometimes get to the destination faster."

Hugging her again, I'm well aware that I'm the one drawing the map.

Maybe I've been quiet, but it's not for any reason that should concern Carter. I take another bite of my pizza with vegetables and mozzarella, and it turns into a devouring-mouthful moment.

It causes Carter to grin. "Hungry?"

I finish my bite and wipe my mouth with my napkin. "More like stockpiling fuel. I'm hungry, but I don't have much room left to actually eat, so the few bites that I manage, I make it count," I explain.

"Solid plan."

The baby shower came and went, and the house is ready.

All the while, my feeling is unbearably strong, and it's time to share it. A silence begins to hang over us, and it causes Carter to shift in his seat.

"I'm going to assume that you've been quiet lately because the approaching labor might feel daunting?"

A smile begins to crawl on my face. "Nah. It's something else."

He stands and offers me his hand. "Come on."

My brows furrow, and I let him lead the way. He tows me to the middle of the living room and spins me straight into his arms, and we begin to sway. We always have background music on when we're eating dinner. And now it seems to help fit his desire to dance.

"What are we doing?" I wonder.

"Dancing." His piercing eyes spear straight into my heart. "We used to do this all the time."

It's true. I would pull him into the middle of the kitchen to dance with me for no reason. "Are you trying to calm me?"

He brings my hand to his chest. "Do I need to?"

That flutter floats inside me again. "No. I'm perfectly relaxed lately." Especially as my thoughts have unraveled into clarity of what was meant to be.

"Good to hear."

Inhaling a deep breath, I'm ready to lay it all on the table. "You know how we managed to forgive our own stupidity, otherwise known as our divorce?" I attempt to throw in some light-heartedness, and I'm thankful when the corner of Carter's mouth shoots up. "Well, I also didn't want to feel as though we needed to have a shotgun wedding because I'm pregnant."

"I get that. However, that's not why I want that ring back on your finger," he assures me.

My fingers resting on his shoulders curl into his shirt.

"But I also wouldn't want to marry because I'm caught in an emotional moment when we meet our child."

Carter cocks his head to the side, and his eyes have a glint of curiosity as he searches for a clue in my own eyes. "Where are you going with this?"

"We've had a quickie wedding once, and this time I'm pregnant and it's kind of the cherry on top."

He doesn't blink. "Again, what are you trying to say?"

The magnetism surrounding us is heavy.

"Carter, I want you to slide the ring back on my finger because I'm ready. I do want to get remarried. I've never been more certain." My entire body feels lighter.

What happens next is a blur, and the only thing keeping me grounded is Carter's lips on mine. A confirming approval. Hard until he brushes his mouth side to side. He hooks his finger under my chin and steals my view, but then he abruptly drops his hand and whisks off in a hurry, leaving me standing in confusion.

The sound of him thumping up the steps fills my ears, followed by heavy feet on the upstairs floor. Blinking a few times, Carter returns downstairs at the rate of a shooting rocket.

Holding up the rings, I chuckle under my breath.

He pants as he lowers to one knee. "I needed the fucking rings."

"I noticed," I say blankly.

His facial features grow stoic. "Rosie, after everything we've been through, we're only stronger, I promise. I'm asking you again and for the last time. Will you marry me?"

I touch the sides of his face because I need to feel him, and I grin at him. "Hmm, let me consider." I toy with him as I draw out the moment. Faltering, I nod. "Yes!"

I pray that the ring still fits around my finger because

everything seems bigger on my body. Luckily, the ring wraps around my skin, still a perfect mold.

He bounces up to kiss me, and I throw my arms around him.

Because I'll only ever have one husband in my life, and it's Carter.

20
ROSIE

My pout causes Carter to nearly howl a laugh as we sit up in bed.

Instantly, my jaw hangs low. "What? It's true!"

He shakes his head, annoyed, and encourages me to lie on my side. It's morning, and it's been snowing steadily since I woke up an hour ago.

"Rosie, I *do* still find you attractive."

"Really? Could have fooled me," I say, flippant.

He scoots closer and wraps his arm around me. Not that he can fit me in his safety net anymore, I'm not getting any smaller. Even since the other day when I requested my ring to return to my finger.

"I'm desperate to fuck you," he breathes into my ear, and his finger begins to circle my clit. "Your tits drive me crazy, and all I want to do is touch you."

I growl a sound because I'm frustrated. "But you won't fuck me."

The feeling of soft lips dusting the curve of my shoulder sends sensitive ripples straight to my sensitive breasts.

"Rosie, putting my cock inside of you right now… scares me. Nothing to do with your amazing beauty, I'm just scared to hurt you."

I wrap my fingers around the wrist of the hand between my legs, and I put in the effort to guide him even lower.

His gravelly morning voice chortles softly into my ear again. "I'm not changing my mind."

"You know some people fuck to get a baby out," I remind him with an annoyed tone.

The pad of his finger stroking my bundle of nerves isn't bad. I mean, I guess, his mouth now circling my nipple isn't horrible either.

"You said it yourself, you have been feeling a bit tighter down there," he says against my skin before he licks the tip of my nipple.

Ah hell, maybe he's right.

I sigh and sink into the mattress as my soon-to-be husband relaxes me in the best possible way. Closing my eyes, he continues his quest while I moan as he takes the speed of his finger up a notch.

It doesn't take long, and he still gets me to what was my end goal to begin with. Blissfully at ease due to an orgasm.

I glance back and give him a kiss. When we part, he is smirking to himself. He feels he has won this little debate. And hell, he might have a few solid points. Everything is starting to feel drastically different.

Carter slips out of bed, still in his boxer briefs because he needed to keep a safety layer between our skin-to-skin contact. His fingers ruffle his hair, and I enjoy the view. Morning Carter is always determined and ready for the routine of his day.

Wobbling out of bed, I make it to the dresser to grab a warm sweater dress to wear around the house. "Do you really have to go? They say the snow will only get heavier as the day goes on. They are expecting a lot of lake effect snow up near Chicago."

He is already buttoning the shirt of his uniform when we look to one another. "I'll only be a few hours. Just think. Soon, I'll be a man always in sweaters and jeans, smiling with prized farm animals." Half of his mouth curves up.

Glancing down to my belly, I rub a circle. "Hear that, little boy or girl? Your daddy is excited to be talking to farm animals. And as First Lady of Everhope, I'll be smiling right there next to him."

Carter walks to me and places a kiss on my forehead. "Not quite First Lady yet."

I hum a sound and finish buttoning his shirt up to his collarbone. "Tomorrow, I will be."

"I'll pick up our license on my way home later and confirm again that we will be meeting with the judge tomorrow. Just a quick signature. It's not our first time at this rodeo."

"Perfect. Just in time before our little bo—" My voice drags, and I squinch my eyes at Carter, seeing if he will slip yet.

He smiles at me. "Little baby," he corrects me.

"Fine," I snap. Maybe I'm a little grumbly today. I just feel lethargic and heavy.

He sets both of his hands on my shoulders to steady me, and his handsome eyes remind me of everything right in my life. I'm where I'm supposed to be.

With him.

Which is why we're getting married.

"You make me so incredibly happy. You know that, right?"

My lips press together and slide to the side. "I do."

He rubs my arms, and his eyes have a tint of marvel as he surveys my body. "I promise. I'll be fast, and tomorrow, we'll sign off on being married… again." He smiles wryly.

"You had to remind us of the again part, didn't you," I tease.

Carter lifts a shoulder before he steps back. "Meh."

After we both finish getting dressed, we head downstairs where Carter fills his to-go coffee mug, and I make chai tea.

"Not stopping at Foxy Rox for your free coffee and muffin? You have them wrapped around your finger, while us peasants are forced to pay full price plus tax." I shake my head in good humor.

He tightens the lid on his cup. "Wish I could, but I think I saw on my morning scroll of the socials that they closed today due to the storm."

I gawk at Carter. "See? All the more reason that you shouldn't be on the road. I swear, I've always had a twinge of fear every time you've ever put on that uniform, although it is kind of hot. Something could happen to you from a crime, even if we live in Everhope. But this snowstorm? Yeah, something doesn't feel right about this."

"Have you been reading your tarot cards again?" He looks at me oddly and is still trying not to laugh.

"No! I don't read tarot cards." I'm offended, and I roll a shoulder back. "It was this week's horoscope. We're in the month of Aquarius," I correct him.

He rolls his eyes at me. "Really. I'll be back. Take a nap or double-check the baby clothes for the thousandth time. Maybe cook a nice meal that we can enjoy together before we have nights of baby crying."

I lift my spoon from my tea and throw it across the kitchen, and it lands in the sink. Least I didn't accidentally hit Carter. "Nice. I made it."

"Look at us, already living our domesticated life as husband and wife." The way Carter approaches me as a man hunting for his prey is causing my body to heat again. "That's what happens when your mommy makes wise decisions," he says to the baby.

"Daddy forgot that the wisest decision was forgetting to use a condom because now we are having you, and we love you already," I coo to my stomach.

Carter chuckles again and quickly kisses my lips. "Rest."

I shoo him away. "Yeah, yeah, yeah."

———

Slowly waking up from my nap on the couch, I adjust to the feeling of a cramp around my waist. I wince as I begin to sit up on my arms, and the throw blanket slips down to my waist. A deep exhale and the feeling subsides.

My eyes roam the living room and fully adjust to my surroundings. I sit up and saunter my way to the window where the snow is still falling, heavier even. Rubbing my eyes, I search for my phone and notice it on the coffee table. One glance and I see that it's almost three.

Carter said a few hours. I guess a few hours could range from one to six. Is that a few?

Feeling awake and energized, I push the thought of the cramp to the side. That is until five minutes later and another one hits. It's bearable, nothing difficult, maybe even easy peasy. It passes and is forgotten.

But okay, this isn't a good sign.

I grimace because I'm not sure if this is funny or scary.

These definitely are contractions, which means it's time, and, of course, Carter isn't here.

I set the stopwatch on my phone and begin to dim the

lighting, light a few candles, and set the mood for a calm beginning of labor that I most definitely was not planning for today.

But panicking won't get me anywhere. Carter will be home soon, and I have no plans to alert him and freak him out. Besides, it's early in the labor, with plenty of time between contractions. We're fine.

I continue arranging the living room for nature's adventure and ready for Carter's return to help me. Then when we feel it's time to go to the hospital, we'll go.

Except half an hour passes and no sign of Carter, but the time between contractions has gone down to four minutes. It causes me to travel from level calm to *hmm, this doesn't feel great*.

I breathe through another contraction, and it's a little more painful than before. It passes, and I can no longer be in denial. Pressing Carter's number on my phone, he picks up after two rings.

"Yeah, so, you need to get home *now*."

"What?"

"Carter, I'm in labor. Baby didn't like our plan of getting married before they enter the world. I thought we had another week. But then I looked at the moon positions and I wanted to scold myself because it makes total sense, and I should have been more prepared," I ramble and walk to the window to revel in the beauty of snow and the quiet of everyone cozy in their houses.

"Rosie, slow down."

"I'm in labor, and I need you here ASAP."

"Rosie!" he squeaks out.

"You sound more terrified than me. Chill it down a notch. Besides, why aren't you home?"

He curses to himself, and I envision him pinching the

bridge of his nose. "I was about to call you. I'm stuck. There is too much snow on Main Street, and the plows won't get out for another two hours."

Fuck tranquility.

"Carter! No. No. No. I need you *here*."

"Listen to me, call my brother and Hailey or Esme, hell, even my mom. Maybe they can all walk to our place."

I gasp in horror. "First off, no fucking way is your brother going to look down there if this baby wants to come out now. Besides, he and Hailey are away for some hockey celebrity thing, and Esme and Keats are there with them. Gracie is at her parents' for the night. And secondly, are you fucking out of your mind? What would possess you to suggest I call your mom? Besides, she hurt her ankle the other day in racquetball and can't even hobble to her martini table in the living room, let alone through unshoveled snow on the sidewalks. The residents of Everhope Road are failing us right now. Will you just get home *now*?" I admit, I'm getting a little feisty.

I'm not sure if it's my outburst or if it's simply that time is ticking but another contraction waves through my body, and I breathe heavily with Carter on the other end. "Please," I beg as I attempt to inhale a long breath and close my eyes, remembering that I have inner Zen to channel.

"You're doing great," Carter encourages as he patiently waits for the contraction to pass. When it does, he is in action mode again. "Rosie, you need to hang up and call the doctor. I have to figure out a way to get to you, but I won't be there soon. I'll call some other neighbors and see if they can do something." I hear the alarm and concern in his voice.

That little bit of panic inside me now rockets high.

"Are you saying that I might be having a baby alone?" I wail. The sound of scratching on glass snatches my eyes away from the window to the kitchen back door to see Jet covered in snow that is up to his stomach. He must have escaped, as Carter's parents are watching him because his mom's secret love for the dog triumphed on the babysitting front. "Great. A canine answered my distress call." I'm being sarcastic, and I walk to the door to let Jet in.

I'm on the receiving end of hearing Carter's puff of air. "Please hang up and call the doctor."

Letting Jet in, he instantly shakes snow away and begins to follow me around as I sway side to side. "Okay. Just get here soon."

Ending the call, I search my contacts and call the doctor's office. After a two-minute check-in of my timing and pain level, they informed me that I need to call 911 if I feel the labor is progressing faster. Not the most comforting of signs, but I take a few more cleansing breaths and lower myself to the floor on all fours then lean forward to rest against my yoga pillow. I need to gather my thoughts and find my inner strength. Jet is instantly next to me, and he must sense my current state, as his nose prods my arm to pet him.

Swallowing and trying to draw in my composure, I admit that I'm struggling. Gritting my teeth through another contraction, I can no longer ignore the facts.

There will be no re-marriage signature tomorrow.

This baby is coming.

And I'm all alone.

21
CARTER

The snowflakes sting every time they melt on my skin as I trudge through the snow that now reaches just below my knees. I'm doing my best to get home, but I'm moving at a snail's pace. I could say that I'm focusing all of my energy on moving, but that would be a lie.

Pure adrenaline and panic have me pushing to work as hard as I can to reach Rosie. My phone battery died right after she called me back to say that she is trying to remain calm, has set the mood with candles, and she'll phone 911 again if she needs to deliver. Not one single thing in that fucking sentence has helped ease my mind.

The moment she hung up, I began my trek, which I can imagine is the same as climbing Everest. I shouldn't have gone in to work, nor left her when she is so far in her pregnancy, but I did, and now there are consequences for my choices.

Rosie has to be okay, and I'm hoping the pain isn't as bad as they say. Selfishly, I don't want to miss seeing our child enter the world. There are so many reasons why I need to ignore how my muscles are beginning to ache from the weight of the fresh powdered snow around my shins and the gusts of wind that sets me back a few steps. Right now, I would play the privileged card if I could. None of it will work, though. The entire town has come to a standstill until the snowfall stops.

On a good day, the walk from our house to Main Street is twenty minutes. Right now, five of those minutes have turned to twenty already. I need to move faster, but I can't.

Keeping my gloved hands stuffed in my pockets, I continue my journey with my heart pounding. The sound of a very slow Jeep catches my attention, and when I glance up ahead on the road, a speck of relief hits me, only to be refilled with adrenaline by the urgency of my situation.

I really fight the resistance of my body trudging against the wind to walk onto the street that is slippery. Managing to grab the man's attention by waving my arm, the driver stops his Jeep, which has chains on the wheels. He keeps the emergency blinking lights on and opens the driver's side door to look down at me.

Close enough, we both get a glimpse of one another through our coats and hats.

"Sheriff Carter?" Pete Smythe, my former opponent, seems to be confused.

I waste no time assessing that he is out in the snow, which isn't surprising considering the guy chases tornados for a hobby.

Ignoring answering his obvious question, I cut to the chase. "You're able to drive?"

"Slowly but surely." He pats the steering wheel with pride. "Got this baby over the summer and can handle all extremes."

"I'm not going to question this. I'm getting in." I begin to circle the Jeep and open the passenger door and hop in.

The moment the door closes, Pete looks at me as he starts the engine up again. "Why are you out here, *Mayor* Carter."

"Drive," I bite out.

"Where to? I heard the plows started out on the east side."

"To my house. Rosie is in labor." My eyes search up ahead at the road to see if I'm giving myself false hope to get to her faster.

His eyes grow bold. "Say no more. I'll get this bad boy up to twenty."

Warming my hands, I do it more to stay occupied.

"First kid, right? We're not supposed to say this as fathers, but the first birth is special, as everything is new. The second child you know what's coming."

"Well, I won't even see the first if I don't get there," I grind out. My eyes scan the vehicle for a plugin. "Do you have a USB cord to charge my phone?"

"Sure thing, I even have enough water for the week under the backseat in case the apocalypse comes. The cord's right in the dashboard." There was zero sarcasm in that sentence because I'm well aware he stocks up on canned goods at the superstore near the highway.

I jerk out the line only to curse to myself, as it has the wrong end to fit into my phone. Someone upstairs is really testing me. Sighing, I sink back in my chair and try to remind myself that there is nothing I can do right now.

"I would say use my phone, but the signal has been iffy all afternoon." Pete indicates with his head to his cell resting in the cupholder as he focuses on the road.

I yank it free and see there are no bars of signal. Angling the phone in different positions, I realize that it's hopeless. Then a dreaded fear pings in my heart that Rosie wouldn't be able to answer anyhow because she's on the phone with the emergency services to help her.

Glancing to my side, I want to appreciate how Pete is happy-go-lucky and whistling a tune from West Side Story, but it doesn't at all help me stay collected. Maybe he notices my grumbly face.

"It's best if you try and remain unruffled. You'll need your strength to help. Whether you miss the labor or not, the next few days will be life-changing. She'll need you." He offers his advice, and since he has five kids, then it can't be too far off the track.

"I won't miss the delivery." I'm defiant.

He doesn't reply, instead we steadily keep driving. I'm paying no attention until he begins to slow to a stop.

"What are you doing? We have to keep going," I insist.

"We're at the end of Everhope Road. You're going to have to walk the rest. One of your neighbors has horrible parallel parking skills and is taking half of the street. I won't be able to get this beast through."

I can do this. Squinting my eyes, I even see a neighbor or two up ahead shoveling while their kids play in the snow.

I nod to him in understanding. "Okay. Thank you." Opening the door, I hop out.

"You've got this," he calls out.

"When I need to appoint city council president then you will be the first I recommend," I say then shut the door.

Guessing the position of the sidewalk, I begin my quest to get home. At moments it feels like dead weight on my ankles, and other times my calves ache from balancing my weight on my feet to avoid falling.

"Hey there, Sheriff Carter. What are you doing out here? Shouldn't you be with Rose?" A neighbor, Kelly, is shoveling the end of her driveway, with her hood nearly covering her entire face, as her son who is a freshman is busy arranging something by the garage.

"I didn't realize you were home. Hopefully, Rosie messaged the neighborhood app. She's in labor."

She adjusts the end of the shovel. "She did, but then she sent a picture to all of us with candles and floor cushions saying that she was perfectly fine and finding her inner tranquility and you would be home any moment."

Well, I'll give Rosie credit for her extreme optimism.

My eyes blaze, and determination to get to my stubborn almost wife again now has reached epic proportions. "Do I look like I'm at home any moment?" I deadpan.

Kelly frowns, and her face screams sympathy. "Okay. Let me think... Snowmobile!"

"What?"

"Jay, bring out your snowmobile. The sheriff or mayor or whatever we are calling Carter these days needs it."

"But Mom, I'm supposed to be meeting my crew down by the parking lot at the river," he complains.

"You don't have *a crew*. You live in Everhope. Now move it," she chides then brings her hand to her heart. "I'll re-text the neighborhood group and tell them that we were given false information about someone's labor. But good news." She splays out her hands as I stare at her blankly. "We already started making a list of who is delivering meals which days for the next two weeks for the new parents."

She seems to grasp that it doesn't feel like good news right now. Our eyes swing to her son tugging his snowmobile out of the garage. He seats himself behind the handlebars and scoots forward. "On ya go, Sheriff. Does this mean I won't get in trouble for not having an updated safety education certificate?"

"Yes!" I get on behind him. "Now let's go."

Kelly begins to jump in place and clap her hands. "Good luck!"

"Let's roll." Jay revs up the engine, and I have to find my bearing as my upper body wobbles.

It doesn't even take thirty seconds for me to realize that this kid should *not* be driving a snowmobile. The engine sound thrums in my ears, the snow feels like stones against my face, and the speed is questionable but gets the damn job done.

He barely stops before I jump off the snowmobile when it slows at the front of my house.

"Good luck," he calls as I'm nearly leaping over snow. I ignore where he zooms away. I barrel through the front door.

"Rosie!"

The sound of a long grunt from upstairs informs me of exactly where I need to go. Skipping two steps at a time as I throw off my coat and gloves, I follow the sound straight to our bedroom.

Then I stop.

My head tilts and my brows furrow.

Candles are lit all around the room, there is the smell of lavender, rose, or jasmine or what the fuck hitting my nose, and background sounds of singing bowls play. There are cushions on the floor with beaded bracelets scattered around. There is also Jet with his chin resting on his paws where he's lying on the floor.

Then there is my wife.

Past and future.

The warrior if I ever knew one.

She's leaning forward against the wall in a tank dress, with one leg bent slightly to the side. She seems to be coming down from a contraction. The phone at her feet with a timer feels like decoration.

"Rosie… I'm here," I tell her as calmly as I can, and I walk to her and touch the curve of her warm shoulder.

Relief and a giant smile instantly spread on her face. "You're here." She sounds breathless.

I smooth back her hair and kiss her forehead. "I'm not going anywhere."

"That's good," she cries. "Because I'm only a minute apart now."

Reminding myself that a soothing voice is what she needs right now, I speak to her. "That's, uh… quite close… perhaps a little too close for comfort… How about we call the emergency services again?"

"Hmm, maybe you're right." She sighs wistfully.

I can't help but explore the scene in front of me and Jet who just perked his head up. Rosie notices and scoffs a laugh.

"I wanted to set the mood, and don't you dare give Jet that look. He's channeling his inner therapy-dog abilities."

Even now, when we should both be petrified out of our minds, she causes us to laugh.

Caressing the sides of her face, I kiss her forehead again. "Why are you so calm?"

"I wasn't. At first, I freaked out in panic. But then, I accepted this is what it is, and I knew deep down that you would be back. So, I set the mood and didn't want anyone to ruin my aura."

Only Rosie would do this.

"Honestly, I don't think I'm so relaxed about it anymo—" She wails as another contraction washes through her body. Rosie grips my arms and squeezes tightly as she works through the contraction.

"Exhale, you're doing great." I'm fairly confident telling her to breathe is more for me than her, because it feels far too simple to say considering what she seems to be going through.

The wave floats away, and her short contraction is gone.

"We can't do this here." She closes her eyes and purses her lips to breathe. "In this room, I mean. But we have no choice."

I support her arms only for her to swat me away, and she drops down in some odd deep squat. Jet goes to stand by the door and watches us. He seems to refuse to leave.

"What the hell are you doing? Now isn't the time for yoga!"

She grips my wrists and pulls. "It's malasana, and it will fucking help get this baby out. He or she needs to feel gravity," she snaps.

I blow a raspberry.

"Ohhh ahh." Rosie struggles again. The contractions seem to be short but closer together. "Carter, gahh." She leans forward to all fours, and I lower to give her the opportunity to lean her head against my shoulder. "There is no way around this. We're having a baby here."

Her honesty sucks the air out of my body, and she stalls to ensure our eyes connect in understanding.

"Please," she begs softly. "Just make this stop," she whispers.

My thumb swirls a circle on her cheek. "You're almost there. I'm going to wash my hands and grab towels, hot water too because I think I heard that once," I answer her. "Can you crawl to the bathroom? It might be a better spot."

She nods in understanding. "Delivering a baby in our bathroom. Okay, we can do this." She pants. Then she weeps. "I don't think I can." She stalls when she begins to move.

Rosie's worn out and struggling, I can read it all over her body.

Cupping her face in my hands, I force her to lock our gaze. Her hair is damp, a sheen of sweat on her face, and still, she's beautiful. "You can do this. I promise you, it will be okay. I'm going to call 911 now," I inform her quietly. "We are going to have our little girl right here," I rasp and admit the truth in hopes it encourages her to stay strong.

Her eyes light up, and a smile begins to curve on her lips with fresh tears in her eyes. "A girl?"

I grin at her. "Yeah… we're having a daughter."

She manages to swat me despite being completely washed out. "You kept it from me all this time."

"You wanted me to! Now, I don't think we should debate this. I'll be quick."

I help her to her knees to the side of the tub for support. Just in time, as another contraction hits. "Hurry! She's here. I feel it. Ahh."

Fuck.

I quickly go into action mode and grab clean towels from the side and snatch her phone from the other room and dial the emergency services.

The woman says hello and recognizes my voice right away, and I don't have time to hear the rest of her spiel.

"She's in labor. Yes, I have towels. And I'm calm." The last part isn't quite true, but I deal.

"Okay, Sheriff, I'm going to dispatch help. The plows have started, so they will get there, but most likely not on time. Be prepared and have a shoestring or string nearby." Well, the lace on my shoe will have to do. "Can you see a head?"

Rosie's eyes turn to saucers when she glances over her shoulder at me. "Oh, no, no, no. If you look down there, Carter, then we will never have a normal sex life again."

"I don't think we have much choice, sweetheart," I grind out with a tight smile.

Rosie can't refute because she's now beginning to push. I get on my knees as Rosie is kneeling. I look and it's a whole different world than what I'm used to, but there are no mistakes. "Yes, I see a head."

"Okay, sir, let her push naturally, it might take a few times."

"Come on, you've got this," I encourage Rosie.

She grits out a long breath and winces as she pushes.

"Our daughter's head is almost there."

"Sheriff, be ready to support the baby, and have a towel nearby."

Rosie gathers her breath before she pushes again. I wish I could hold her, but too much is happening between her legs that she parts wider open for the next two pushes.

"One last push or I swear to mother earth—" Rosie's muffled sounds to accompany her long push lead us to our destination.

It feels as though I'm catching our daughter in a towel. It's a brief moment before the sound of a cry fills the room.

"Sheriff, check the baby's mouth and nose. Use your fingers if needed."

But our daughter is healthy. Rosie moves to sit on the floor, and I hand her our little girl wrapped in a towel.

I don't care about any fluid all over my hands or floor because Rosie and I both are in awe of our little girl who lies against her chest.

"She's beautiful." Rosie peers down.

"Yeah… she is," I lament

Jet barks from the other room, and I forgot that he was here, but I hear him run away. The rest is a blur of what the operator says or when the paramedics arrive.

I'm completely in love with the two girls in my life.

22
ROSIE

Sighing in contentment, I sit up in the hospital bed the morning after our adventure. Carter hands me our daughter, and we both have ridiculous smiles on our faces.

"Here is our little princess for her breakfast." He sits on the edge of the bed and has no intention of leaving. I smirk at him as I adjust our daughter at my chest. He steals a glimpse of the sign that says Baby Cassidy Oaks. We'll call her Cassie to incorporate Carter's and my name. It begins with his and ends with mine.

We're doing great after getting checked out. Truthfully, if it wasn't for the hospital band around my wrist then I would say we could have just stayed home after this little bundle of ten toes and fingers came into the world. It's unbelievable how this all transpired.

It still hasn't registered that we are parents. It's only the little gurgles that remind us of the fact.

I notice Carter's smug smirk. "What are you up to?" I wonder then glance down at our daughter who is holding onto my crooked pinky.

Carter brushes the side of his hand gingerly across Cassie's hair. "I have a surprise for you, but only if you want it."

The corner of my mouth stretches. "Why wouldn't I want a surprise? Oh yeah, because then I go into labor unexpectedly," I remark.

"Okay, this surprise is more news."

"That our parents won't be here for another hour?" I look at him, intrigued but confused.

He laughs and rubs my leg. "The roads did clear." He shrugs. "But that also means I can use an almost-mayor perk and the judge can stop on by… if you want." Carter quirks his lips out and plays casual.

I sputter a laugh. "You mean to get married?" He nods. "Here?" He nods again. "As in, I'm washed out with a baby in my arms, but hell, let's just knock out all life events in a twenty-four-hour period?"

Carter's palms fly up to ease me. "Your choice."

Sighing, I can't help but smile at our little girl. "Your daddy is really putting me on the spot, you know that, right?"

"It was supposed to be our wedding today," he points out. "The whole married before she's born idea went out the window, but the sign-off on us can still happen."

I point to the little hat on the bedside table, and like clockwork, Carter grabs it and positions it on Cassie's head.

"Thanks. We need to cover her ears to prevent her from hearing me burst out laughing," I explain dryly as my smile begins to creep across my face.

"A perk of being married twice to one another is that I can read you. It seems that I should be speed-dialing someone," he gloats, and I roll my eyes because he's right.

"So unfair. I don't even have mascara with me." Although I love my post-labor pajamas. A little lace over gray cotton tank and long pants with fuzzy socks. Gracie gave the outfit at my baby shower.

Carter takes that as an answer, and I'd be lying if it wasn't the cue to my reply. He stands and fishes his phone out of his pocket. "I'll call him then."

Now I'm amused with this spontaneous development of our day. "What about our family that is about to descend upon us?"

"Your call. I can either tell them to wait once they get here while the judge does his thing or they come in here with no clue."

My eyes grow wide. "Are you crazy? The whole hospital will hear our moms lose their cool." I consider that for a moment. "I mean... if they're here anyways, then we might as well." I brush it off as though it's no big deal.

The sound of Carter's chuckle won't be forgotten in my entire life. "I was not expecting that little plot twist."

"What?" I'm ready to defend myself. "Cassie has the same trait. We like the element of spontaneity."

He quickly steps to us and leans down to kiss our foreheads. "I'll go make the call," he whispers.

Staring down at the squinched little face who doesn't understand the new world that she is in, I just want to cuddle in her cuteness. "Your daddy can be grumpy, demanding, and then out of nowhere, be far too confident and euphoric."

A knock on the door before it cracks open raises my attention to see Hailey and Oliver peeking in. "Ready for visitors?" Hailey asks.

"Come on in."

The moment the door fully opens, a giant balloon on a string that says *beary excited to meet you* appears, along with a fruit basket and a bag with tissue paper.

Hailey is cooing and approaching us with vigor. "She's so adorable."

Oliver is a little more reserved and gives us a little distance. "My little niece didn't make it easy for you guys, did she?" He goosenecks to get a glimpse, but his wife is stealing the view. "I heard you had a guest at the event, too. Supervising so that my brother wouldn't mess up."

"Hey! Already? Can't give me five minutes before the sarcasm hits?" Carter chides his brother as he joins us again in the room.

"He might be right," I tease Carter. "Dogs can detect labor, apparently. He loves grumpy Carter so much that he came to save me. Don't worry, guys, we gave him a treat from Carter's hidden treat jar as a reward for his efforts."

The lighthearted conversation continues as everyone comments on our beautiful little girl that we gush over.

"We kind of need your help if you don't mind. It's the least you can do for being away when we needed a neighbor the most," Carter impassively reprimands.

"Excuse us for having a life. We got back as soon as we could. What can we do?" Oliver responds.

Carter and I smirk at one another.

"Keep our parents in line when they get here," Carter requests.

Hailey laughs. "Not happening. The first grandchild is in the room, but I give you a point for optimism."

"Gotta support my wife on that one," Oliver adds.

"Fine. Can you at least meet the judge in the lobby to show him to our room?"

Oliver's face puzzles, then he swims his eyes side to side. "Ah. Legal talk. Are you two getting hitched? Shotgun wedding kind of thing?"

Hailey squeals and brings her hands together. "Ooh, a wedding."

"Yeah, keep that on the down-low until everyone is here and the judge just randomly shows up," Carter implores.

"Love easygoing weddings," she comments.

Carter points to the door. "Great. Now you two go and get to work."

Oliver shakes his head in amusement. "They're kicking us out already."

"All good. I've arrived bearing gifts." My sister Bella peeks around the door.

"We'll be back, so get in line on the baby-holding list." Hailey indicates with her fingers that she's watching Bella.

"You two are already leaving?" Bella asks, perplexed, as she holds a big Labrador stuffed animal.

"We have an important mission," Oliver explains in passing.

Carter circles the bed to lift Cassie out of my arms to let her rest in the hospital bassinet It will be easier for everyone to see her.

I stifle a laugh. "Did you choose that stuffed animal to remind Carter of who was present at the birth of our daughter?"

"Totally." My sister has no qualms stating the obvious as she joins me on the bed.

The next few minutes, we chat and go over the details of the night before.

We don't even need to check the door when we hear both sets of parents walking down the hall.

"Twenty bucks that Dad says he can't handle the grandpa title," she mutters under her breath to me as she straightens her back and stands up to go hide in the corner.

Carter winces as he scrubs a hand across his stubbled jaw and remains close to our daughter.

We all watch the door fling open when our parents pile through with flowers, wrapped presents, and a basket of baby clothes. I couldn't even say what belongs to whom because they all blob together.

"My baby has a baby." My mom is victorious on reaching me first and leans down to give me a big hug with tears in her eyes. "You did so well." Then she playfully pinches my shoulder. "Don't ever have a baby during a snowstorm again," she scolds me.

"Speak to your granddaughter about that," I remind her and smile.

My dad is quick to lean over and hug me. "I'm not sure I'm liking this grandpa title, I'm not getting that old."

I glance to the corner where Bella sticks her thumb up. Then the next set of parents hug me in congratulations before everyone circles around our little marvel. Swinging my legs out of bed, I walk over to join them, and our little girl should probably be wailing at the top of her lungs right now with all of these new faces, but instead, she is calm and basking in the attention she isn't aware that she's receiving.

Nancy has her hands on her heart. "What a little darling. I'll babysit you, yes, I will." The voice that we all harbor comes out in full force. The type of voice that is an octave too high and so incredibly joyful.

"And she will have such a fun time at Olive Owl when *I* will babysit," my mom corrects her, and I roll my lips in to hide my laugh.

"I have cigars, Son." Edward slaps a hand on Carter's shoulder. He never struck me as a man who loved cutesy moments with babies or animals.

The door cracks open, and Oliver gives Carter a thumbs-up.

"Well, Dad. Hopefully your brought extra cigars."

My dad pipes up but continues to be enamored by Cassie. "No worries. I brought my own."

Oliver enters with Hailey and the judge, an older man I've seen a few times at the grocery store.

"Judge Daniels, what are you doing here?" Edward draws everyone's attention to our new arrival.

Before the judge can say anything, Carter comes to side-hug me. "If we just bang out the two-minute version then we're okay, right?" he asks me offhandedly as though nobody is here.

I ignore that anyone is in the room as I reach down to swoop our daughter up into my arms. "Yeah, that's fine. I'll just pick her up."

"What's… what's going on?" My mother is as bewildered as everyone else.

"Just getting married again. It will be like two minutes," I explain coolly.

Her eyes flutter as my dad tries to catch up, and Nancy's jaw just dropped.

Carter's hand rests on my lower back, and he smiles at the judge. "Let's get this done. If we're lucky, we'll be done before their freakout ends."

"Oh, I heard that." Bella is not impressed. She pulls a flower out of the bunch in a vase and saunters to me to offer the light pink rose to me. "Here. Be a bride even though you never told me." Now, she's just throwing on theatrics.

I lift my arm slightly to support Cassie's head. "No flowers. I'm holding precious goods."

"Fine. I'll hold onto it as your maid of honor."

"Self-appointed title, but fine, okay, sure," I say dryly, but I'm still happy as a clam.

"Can't *any* of my sons get married in a normal way? Preferably not hiding the fact from all of us until they decide not to?" Nancy shakes her head.

Oliver holds his hands up in the air. "Hey, not my fault Carter decided to take a very smart move from my book."

"Or we can refresh everyone's minds that Rosie and I were married once before, so we just need to hash out a few details to re-marry. So if you could all give us a second, maybe debate whose flowers are better arranged, as Rosie and I have something to do." Carter glances to me with warmth and assurance on his face.

I grin widely because this is all perfect. Every single second, from a snowstorm to the bathroom floor, to our little girl in our arms, and a quickie wedding that catches everyone by surprise. You couldn't imagine a better twenty-four hours.

"Let's just go for it," Carter instructs the judge.

"Oh, so we're really doing this here?" My mom points to the ground.

"Yep." I tighten the P.

There is a brief silence in the room before everyone jolts into realization that we're not joking.

"Someone film this." Nancy elbows Edward to get his phone out. "Thank goodness there is a bottle of champagne in the basket."

"Or we have a bottle of Olive Owl wine in the car," my dad mutters.

Carter clears his throat. "Uh, Judge. Let's start."

He looks bewildered at everyone in the room and smiles nervously but returns his gaze to Carter. "Of course."

The judge steps closer in our direction, as Carter and I have our daughter in our arms.

"We are gathered here today…" the judge begins.

"We can keep moving," I suggest.

"Do you, Rosalyn Blisswood, take Carter Oaks to be your lawfully wedded husband?"

I smile brightly, and my eyes meet Carter's in recognition that I'm confident and ready for this. "Yes, I do… again."

"And do you, Carter Oaks, take Rosalyn Blisswood to be your wife?"

He squeezes me closer to his body. "I do… again."

"Do you two have vows?"

Awkwardly, I chuckle. "Well, we'll skip those. This little girl speaks volumes as to why we maybe don't need vows. She's symbol enough of our actions."

"Rosie!" I hear my dad tsk from the side.

"Chillax," my sister tells them. "It's obvious what it takes to make a baby, and it's their wedding."

The judge's brows rise, and I'm sure this will go down as one of his most unconventional weddings.

"Okay, so no vows. Rings?"

Carter and I hold up our fingers. "All good from the last round."

"You've made this a little too easy for me."

"That's not them, but okay, we'll play along," Oliver states from the corner of the room and pretends to look away.

The judge smiles at everyone. "Well then. By the authority vested in me in the state of Illinois, I pronounce you husband and wife. You may kiss your bride."

Faintly, I hear the sounds of our family saying something, but I take no notice because Carter leans down until our foreheads touch.

"We can just forget the little blip that we were ever unmarried," he whispers.

"We're all mended now," I promise.

His lips brush along mine, a mix of heat and a tickle, only soothed by his lips planting a soft kiss on my mouth. It's nothing wild but powerful and sentimental. Pulling away, I can imagine the sparkle in his eyes must match a glimmer in my own.

And right on cue, our daughter begins to fuss before a full shrieking cry breaks out.

23

CARTER

SIX MONTHS LATER

Rosie gives me *that* look. The one where she knows that a quick hello with someone will turn into a five-minute conversation, and every single time, she smiles to herself with pride. Now, she's sitting by the window at Foxy Rox with our beautiful little daughter sitting up on her lap and gnawing on a rubber duck because the teething era is a bitch.

I turn my attention to Sara who owns Foxy Rox; I haven't been ignoring her. She's young and a small entrepreneur. "I agree," I continue our conversation. "If state taxes increase, then we'll have to see about city tax and what we can do to even it out for small businesses. It's on the agenda for the next meeting. Feel free to attend to present your concerns."

She sighs. "Thanks, Mayor Carter. I'm sorry to be keeping you from Rose and Cassie."

"It's fine." I throw her an assuring look.

She waves me off. "Well, you go back to your table, and I'll bring you guys a piece of cake on the house."

Perks of being mayor. "Can't say no to that."

As I'm nearly at the home plate of my seat at the table, with a coffee waiting for me, Rosie raises her brows and smirks to herself as her lips wrap around the rim of her teacup.

"Mayor Carter." A new deep voice greets me.

I repaint a polite smile on my face as I side turn to see Sam, a local farmer. "Good to see you."

He shakes my hand and nods a hello to Rosie. The middle-aged man has his hat tucked under his arm. "Just wanted to check if you've heard the news about Bessy."

Licking my lips, I grin to myself because his first pride is his animal, not his son. "Of course, who in Everhope hasn't. Great to hear that your son won in the junior livestock over at the Sandwich Fair. Goats, right?"

"Yeah. You'll be coming around for pictures? You can bring the whole family. We have a new litter of puppies, too." He's proud as he should be.

"I'll be there next Tuesday, I believe. That's what the office told me."

"See you then. Sorry to interrupt." He offers Rosie one more smile before he scurries away to the counter.

Finally sitting down, Rosie now grins at me.

Dragging a hand across my jaw, I soak in that my wife is always right. "What?" I shrug.

She stabs a fork into a piece of carrot cake that must have arrived during my conversation. "Nothing." She's playing coy. "Just…" she adds, appearing puzzled to the mix. "Imagine if someone were to tell you that there is no way you will be left alone for a peaceful cup of coffee at Foxy Rox."

My head bobbles side to side before I throw up my arms in defeat. "Okay, you were right."

Rosie cups her ear. "What was that? I'm not sure I heard you."

A grin stretches my cheeks. "My beautiful wife was right."

She giggles to herself as she shakes Cassie's plastic toy in front of her. We gave up on only wooden toys, handwashed cotton, and classical music when our sleepless states led us to doing whatever possible to survive. "Carter, it's no big deal. You're popular. Every time. Grocery store, park, walks on Main Street," she lists.

I cluck the inside of my cheek. "But Everhope Road's attention is reserved for you, my Mayoress."

All the neighbors love her like crazy. It's either questions about our daughter, advice on yoga or what herbs to burn, and simply Rosie being cheery all the time. The mailman can talk Rosie's ear off sometimes, too.

She snickers a laugh. "It's more like I need to keep our neighbors quiet since this little one probably keeps everyone up."

Our little girl coos and blows a little bubble.

"Cassie's growing, it's expected."

"Is that why your parents put rum on her gums?" she deadpans.

Snorting a laugh, I steal her fork. "It was a rough few hours when they babysat. I mean, she did have a tooth coming in," I attempt to justify the logic.

"Sure." She rolls her eyes.

I indicate with my hand that she can hand our daughter over and I'll hold her. It's an easy tradeoff, and Cassie settles on my lap, and I can't help but notice how Rosie is admiring the view and seems to grow quiet.

"You good?"

She nods and presses a smile. "Very."

Sliding the plate of cake away from me to avoid little curious grabby hands, I remember what we're supposed to be doing today.

"You think she'll last for our grocery-store run?" I wonder.

Rosie lifts her shoulders. "We'll try. I hear there is a sale in the rum section." She winks at me.

My wife's wit has only gotten stronger since she became a mom. Humor and parenthood go hand in hand.

"If we get her down for a nap later, can I pour the rum on you?" My voice is determined, and I hear the undertone of swelter.

She pretends to blush and leans into the table. "Mayor Carter, we're in public. Watch that mouth of yours."

"I would rather have my mouth on you," I volley back.

Her face falls. "Okay, now you need to take it down a notch. There are little ears present, and I'm sure you'll go feral if I tell you that I'm wearing a new matching bra-and-panty set."

Sternly, I give her a warning glare. "We need to get out of here. Get those errands down fast then make it home," I suggest.

She abruptly stands up and gives an over-the-top smile. "I'm in agreement."

An hour later, we have groceries, managed to get through the aisles without anyone stopping us, and instead of getting our daughter down for a nap so her parents can get naked, we find ourselves pushing Cassie's stroller down the sidewalk with the sun still out.

Rosie interlaces her arm with mine as we meander along, and she waves with her other hand at a neighbor watering their plants.

"Are we walking by your brother's?"

"Nah, the dog gets a little too excited around Cassie. Besides, Oliver will suggest we have a BBQ later, and then I'll find myself back at the grocery store."

She gently smacks my arm. "Not everyone gets to have their sibling live close enough that you can borrow milk."

I grin. "I know." It's peaceful, an easy-going afternoon. "Maybe we should check on Esme and Keats."

"Nah, they are in their nesting phase and were going to try and build a diaper table or something today, since the baby is almost here."

We both wince at that thought. "A leisurely afternoon for us then."

Rosie hums, and it sounds blissful. "Perfect."

Leaning over, I get a glimpse of Cassie whose eyes are growing heavy, and in any moment, our mission will be complete, and she'll be asleep. In the corner of my eyes, I can't help but notice how Rosie looks off into the distance.

"Today you seem a little off," I note.

She sighs and brings her head to rest against my arm. "I'm happy. In a good place."

"Is that what your horoscope said today?" I tease her.

"Har-har."

It grows quiet between us again. Only the sound of a sprinkler in someone's yard and birds chirping reminds us that we are outside.

"Sometimes life makes sense."

My brow lifts. "Oh yeah?" I'm intrigued.

"Yeah." Her voice thins. "You and I weren't always simple, but everything I needed to be happy is being with you, living on this road, having our family. I feel complete and right where I'm meant to be."

Those are the words that anybody would want to hear. It's a thousand times better when it's your wife.

I stop us and force her to face me with that usual whimsical mist in her eyes. "Rosie, maybe that's for you. But for me, everything I needed has always been you. The rest is a bonus."

She licks her lips and swallows, visibly struggling to bury a tear. "You're going to make me cry in public, aren't you?"

The faintness of a grin can probably be seen on my lips. "No need to cry if it's the truth."

Nearly throwing herself at me, her hands frame my face, and she crushes my mouth with a kiss. "I love you."

"Love you, too."

She smiles, a tear sliding down her cheek. "Come on, I have wicked ideas."

EPILOGUE: ROSIE

3 YEARS LATER

Counting the paper unicorn plates, I check that we have enough. Between neighbors, Carter's family, and my own family, I'm not quite sure why we didn't have our daughter's third birthday party somewhere else.

"Why is it so difficult for them to hang a banner? Like seriously, they've been at this for five minutes," Esme comments as she stands next to me in the kitchen, holding her toddler. It's nice having kids close in age; playdates and coffee are part of our routine.

Dropping the plates on the counter, I review the scene, and my lips quirk out. She isn't wrong. "It's all about height, I guess?"

"Sure. What's with men and counting inches," she quips.

I chortle a laugh. "Can we keep it PG? It's a birthday party, after all."

She shrugs. "It's true." She passes her son a cracker from

the snack tray. "On a level of one to ten, how chaotic is this party going to be?"

"A nine point five."

Bouncing her son on her hip, she grabs his little hand. "Fun. Now let's go see if Auntie Hailey has delivered that baby yet." She walks away to join Hailey on the couch where she is taking up residence for the party, rightfully so, as she's about to deliver a girl any day now.

Glancing to my sister sitting on the floor with Cassie and playing with her tea set, I make note that Bella has been acting strange all day. I'm about to head their way, but a man with swagger and predatory eyes is approaching me.

"Bravo for finally hanging the decorations," I tease Carter who wraps his arms around me.

"Don't get sassy on me. We already have a little princess over there who gives it to us in full," he reminds me.

I giggle because he is very right. Stepping back, I lean into Carter's shoulder as he stands by my side to observe our daughter squealing in delight. "She's growing too fast."

"We can always do it again," he highlights. We give one another a glance before bursting out a laugh. "Yeah, we're not going there."

I always thought that I would want a big family. The same as I grew up with. However, my views changed after having Cassie. Every day is pure sunshine and lullabies, but it's work and far too many sleepless nights. It's to the point where my imagination has me second-guessing if she is possessed, and I burn sage to save us all. Except, that is not the case. She's healthy, but sleep isn't for her, barely any hours a night since she was born. It affects you when you rarely get a night of rest. It's not a risk we want to take again. Maybe we will change our minds one day, but for now, one kid it shall be.

"It's all good. Just the three of us," I agree, then sigh as our little girl is no longer a baby.

The loss of Carter in my arms brings my attention back to the tasks at hand. He steals a carrot from the tray and evaluates all of the options for snacks.

"Feeding an army?"

I raise my brow because he should know better. "Something like that. It's our families."

"And Jet," Oliver adds as he joins us around the snacks. We all dart our attention to the back French doors to see Jet standing in the snow and wagging his tail. Carter and I have considered many times that we need to get our own dog, but Jet visits us enough. "Cupcakes. Nice choice." Oliver tips his nose to the box of pink icing and sprinkle-covered mini cakes.

"Cookies, too. Options for everyone."

Carter returns to me and slips his arms around my waist from behind. "She thinks of everything, this one." He pulls me close to his body, and for a second, I'm questioning if we are crossing the border on public display of affection.

"Good. One of you needs to have a brain in your relationship," Oliver says in jest to hold up their brotherly camaraderie.

"Aren't you funny. Now make yourself useful and grab the champagne," Carter instructs him with a cheeky smile on his face.

I shake my head because they may be grown men, but they are adorable with one another.

My husband gathers champagne flutes, and Oliver grabs a bottle of champagne and orange juice from the fridge. With supplies in hands, we stroll over to the living room where everyone has congregated.

"A toast before the circus gets here," Carter announces

with that suave grin that makes me molten every single time. It drives the old ladies at town council meetings crazy, too.

"Gotta listen to our mayor." Keats smiles and helps distribute the glasses.

Bella stands to sit on the armrest of the couch and next to Esme who placed her son on the ground to play with Cassie.

"Not fair. I have to resort to orange juice." Hailey is grumbly, and I'm positive she's physically uncomfortable, too.

Carter holds up the bottle. "I know today is for our daughter, but we deserve to celebrate too for surviving three years of hugs, tantrums, and thrown toys. But you gotta love them." He glances over his shoulder to stare down affectionately at our daughter who looks up at him with doe eyes full of wonder and a cute little smile while she holds her stuffed dog. "Yes, we do. We love you," Carter tells her in his special voice reserved for our daughter.

"To good neighbors and friends. Thankfully no snowstorm, either. Thank you for being here." I begin to feel warmth on my face and then a sting at the top of my cheeks as tears swell at the bottom of my eye. "Okay, I'm emotional. My little baby is three, and we're all getting older, and I just want to down some alcohol."

Everyone lets out a chuckle and smiles as we all raise our glasses.

"Thankfully we all live on Everhope Road—"

Oliver intercepts Carter's effort to continue his toast. "Which also means it would be awkward if we turned down the party invite." My husband grins, because as much as Oliver is joking, he raises a valid point.

"As I was saying. To all of us. Thank you for being here and celebrating our daughter's third birthday. Cheers."

Everyone clinks their glasses with whoever is closest before taking a sip.

"Ooh, this is yummy. Where is this from?" Esme studies the liquid in her glass.

"From Olive Owl, it's from my family. I had a crateful in my trunk," Bella explains.

Before Esme can further their conversation, the sound of the front door opening and a herd of people entering the house causes me to down the rest of my glass in one go.

I love our families. I really do. But together? I need all of the strength. Our parents plus singing "Happy Birthday" with cake all over Cassie and everyone insisting on photos. It's going to be a scene, for sure.

"Where is my little grandbaby?" I already hear my mom, as she must be getting her coat and boots off.

I notice that Bella has roamed to the corner of the living room near the windows. She seems a little lost.

Joining her, I nudge her shoulder. "You okay? You seem off."

She smiles weakly at me. "Totally." She brings her drink to her lips, and it seems to be more of an avoidance tactic.

"Could've fooled me," I reply flatly. "Come on, what's up?"

"Don't you have guests to attend to?"

I sputter a laugh. "*Please.* They're not here for me. Besides, when Cassie is in the room then it's like they forget who even lives here with her."

"It's just… everyone is so happy and with someone. Me?" She blows out a breath.

I give her a hug. "Relax. Mr. Right will come."

"All of our cousins will be married before me."

I chuckle and smile at her. "We have a lot of Blisswood

cousins, and to my knowledge, nobody currently has a riveting love life."

Bella looks at me as though I'm crazy. "Are you kidding me? Gracie is pregnant with the hockey coach, not planned." We both swing our gaze to the kitchen where she is chatting with my mom.

"Oh yeah. But still, don't worry."

She gives me a stern look and points her finger at me. "Fine. You're right. Maybe one day. I mean, I might have kind of accidentally broken that no-fraternizing clause that I signed."

This excites me. "Ooh."

"Nothing special. Just a solid make-out session at a holiday party."

There is no possible way to even suppress my jaw dropping and the smile painting on my face. "I live for these details."

"The holidays make everyone a little crazy. I mean, does your kid really need five outfit options?"

"Hey, snowman, reindeer, Santa, elf, and a dreidel ensures she is ready to roll with every single mayoral function and family photo."

She laughs at me. "If those are your concerns, then you're doing fine."

I smile softly to myself and glance at Carter talking to friends with a beer in his hand. Our eyes latch for a second. Yeah. Life is good when you have a loving husband, a daughter who is our joy, and a street we call home. Finally, I have everything I need.

THANK YOU

Getting a book into readers' hands goes beyond my words. It takes more. A big thank you to my readers, editor (Lindsay), cover designer (Lindsey), family, hockey players, coffee, songs on repeat, and Rachel, who keeps me sane 87% of the time.

Made in the USA
Middletown, DE
14 April 2025